D0526179

WITHDRAWN FROM STOCK

Kolya

WITHDRAWN FROM STOCK

Zdeněk Svěrák

Translated from the
Czech by Ewald Osers

LIMERICK COUNTY LIBRARY
G52923

review

KOLYA by Zdeněk Svěrák
Based on the idea by Pavel Taussig
Copyright © Zdeněk Svěrák, 1996
c/o Aura-Pont, Prague
First edition published by PRIMUS, Prague, 1996

English Language Translation Copyright © 1997 Ewald Osers

The right of Zdeněk Svěrák to be identified as the Author of
the Work has been asserted by him in accordance with the
Copyright, Designs and Patents Act 1988.

First published in Great Britain in 1997
by HEADLINE BOOK PUBLISHING

A REVIEW paperback

10 9 8 7 6 5 4 3 2 1

All rights reserved. No part of this publication may be
reproduced, stored in a retrieval system, or transmitted,
in any form or by any means without the prior written
permission of the publisher, nor be otherwise circulated
in any form of binding or cover other than that in which
it is published and without a similar condition being
imposed on the subsequent purchaser.

All characters in this publication are fictitious
and any resemblance to real persons, living or dead,
is purely coincidental.

ISBN 0 7472 5894 5

Typeset by
Letterpart Limited, Reigate, Surrey

Printed and bound in Great Britain by
Clays Ltd, St Ives plc

HEADLINE BOOK PUBLISHING
A division of Hodder Headline PLC
338 Euston Road
London NW1 3BH

Kolya

The string quartet is playing Dvořák. They are clearly enjoying themselves.

The acoustics are good, but it's no concert hall. If it were they'd have more space, the first violin wouldn't have a beer bottle by his left foot, the cellist wouldn't be playing without his shoes on, and behind the second violin there wouldn't be a low stool topped with a blotchy asbestos sheet on which sits an electric hotplate with a kettle from whose spout steam is just beginning to escape.

Of the four musicians, the cellist deserves our main attention, for he is František Louka, our principal character.

Louka's full beard and hair was possibly pepper-and-salt not so long ago, but by now it's nearly all salt which, in point of fact, is finding it difficult to establish itself because his hair is getting thin. If you hazarded a guess at his age you might say fifty-five. But his eyes under his high forehead are very much alive, and so is he generally.

For instance, just now as Dvořák's moving harmonies are pierced as with a needle by the whistle of the kettle, Louka uses a half-bar rest to flick off the whistling spout-piece with an adroit movement of his bow. The whistle rolls across the floor to a pair of court shoes. Rising from them are two rather shapely female legs. And as, curiously, we follow them up we find that the skirt is filled by a solid behind. It belongs to a forty-five-year-old blonde, Klára Koutská. With a sweater flung over her shoulders and her music held at arm's length – she really needs glasses but is too vain to wear any – she begins to sing.

Her well-rounded alto rises to the ceiling, rebounds there, and now drops down all the way to the ears of the handful of mourners who, in the

1

*Take a good look at him, for he is František Louka,
our principal character (Zdeněk Svěrák).*

ceremonial hall of the Strašnice Crematorium, have fixed their moist eyes on a wreath-covered coffin.

The violoncello has another rest. Louka turns his sheet music and, because there are only a few seconds left to him now, reaches out and touches the singer's buttocks which are contracted into unusual tautness by her efforts. This is obviously not the first time he has done this, but it nevertheless catches Klára off guard. Her voice falters for a moment, so much so that the musically more sensitive mourners notice it and exchange questioning glances.

The singer overcomes her vocal wavering and, to be on the safe side, steps out of Louka's reach, but not far enough. When the cello has a few bars' rest the dirty old man uses his bow to raise her skirt higher and higher, which his three colleagues gleefully observe with their peripheral vision, but without Dvořák suffering in the least.

As the piece ends and the coffin jerkily retreats into the cremation chamber, the curtain closes and the musicians pack up their instruments.

The contralto Klára turns round and, looking at Louka who is hurriedly putting his shoes on, sighs: 'You old bugger, will you never grow up?'

And as she threads her way between the musicians she slaps his face, though in a playful rather than hostile fashion.

'Who's for coffee?' asks Pekárek, the first violin, picking up the kettle.

'Me,' says Klára and is joined by the viola player.

'How about you, Franta?'

'No, thanks. I've got to rush off,' answers Louka, putting his bulky instrument into a battered case.

'You're always having to rush off,' says the first violinist, pouring boiling water into a cup. 'You must be raking it in, Louka. One job after another . . .'

'Oh, sure. Jardo, lend me a hundred, till Monday,' Louka begs in a muted voice.

The first violinist examines his wallet and hands him a green one-hundred note.

'You'll get it back,' the cellist assures him, shouldering his case with its strap like a huge bulging gun.

'I know I will. You wouldn't have it otherwise,' the violinist replies while he is dispensing another cup of coffee.

As the door closes behind Louka, Pekárek shakes his head. 'The times we live in. Such a player . . .'

The singer drops a little sweetener pill into her coffee and asks: 'Does anybody know just what he has done?'

The packed tram halts at the Crematorium stop and, even though it looks hopeless, Louka with his big black load forces his way on. The door closes and just the tail of his coat remains trapped outside.

Like a busy beetle, Franta Louka with his black case on his back scurries uphill to the Motoly Crematorium, overtaking groups of sombrely clad people.

From the organ loft under the ceiling comes solemn music.

This time the deceased's family has asked for Fibich's *Poem*.

Out of breath, Louka hastily removes his cello from its case, on his way to the music stand he adjusts the frog on his bow and joins in.

'About time too,' Musil, the organist, greets the latecomer, his short-sighted eyes reproachful over the rims of his thick glasses. Louka plays movingly, the vibrato of his left hand designed to appease his colleague.

In the car park Louka loads his instrument into Musil's Wartburg, still trying to pacify his colleague.

'This is an ideal car, this is. Nice and spacious . . .'

'You should at least get yourself a Trabant,' says Musil, angrily slamming the hatch door. 'Because you're just not coping with that heavy case of yours. Don't take this personally, Franta, but you're just not coping. And there are heaps of cellists about. Not of your calibre, of course, but good enough for funerals. How am I to cover up for you?'

'I know. I'm sorry,' says Louka, getting into the car.

They're driving through late-afternoon Prague. This is the time when the factories pour their employees into the streets. Whole bunches of them are crowding the tram stops. Our cremation musicians are more interested in the female workers. One, who was about to cross to the traffic island in front of them, changed her mind at the last moment and Musil just avoided running her over.

'That one would have been a pity,' says Louka when the brakes have stopped screeching and the girl has run across to the tram with an apologetic smile.

'That's right,' agrees Musil, slipping his glasses off for a moment, breathing on them and wiping them on his jacket lapel.

'Pretty girl,' says Louka, turning his head after her. Then he asks:

'How much is a Trabant these days?'

'New or second-hand?'

'Second-hand.'

'You need a station wagon. Twenty, twenty-five thousand.'

Louka lets out a whistle.

On the right-hand pavement, going in their direction, are three girls in miniskirts. Musil slows down and our two old lechers scan their perfectly ordinary movements from behind as if this were some heavenly vision.

The car behind them flashes its headlights into Musil's rear mirror, irritated by his dawdling.

'I'm moving, aren't I, you nitwit,' the organist answers him and puts his foot down. As the Wartburg passes the three girls Musil turns his head to get a look at them from the front. Instantly he regrets it.

'I tell you the rear view was a lot better.'

'I didn't turn round. For me they remain beautiful. To the end of my days,' Louka laughs.

'Listen, Louka, you used to tour the world with that symphony orchestra. How did you get on with the women there? French women, Italian women, mulattos . . .'

'Not at all. I'm no good at languages. And at the same time I'm a chatter-up. But if you don't know the language, how can you chat them up?'

Musil laughs. 'Except of course in Russia. Want it or not? Is easy in Russian.'

'I'm no good even in Russian, believe me,' says Louka. 'So you're saying twenty thousand? Well, that's out of the question.'

With his instrument on his back Louka climbs the stairs of a house in

Prague's historical Little Quarter. There is now a bottle in his hand, wrapped in paper and a carrier bag with some food. He is out of breath and has to stop for a moment.

'Keeping well, Maestro?' a neighbour in dungarees greets him on his way down.

'Trying to,' Louka replied.

'Coming from a concert, are you? How was it?'

'Terrific,' Franta breathes, more to himself.

'Doing the brake linings,' the man calls up from below.

'Yourself?'

'Sure. I do everything myself.'

On the fourth floor the wide stairs come to an end and the ones leading up to the attic are narrow. Louka continues up.

As he opens the ancient door with its handwritten notice

DON'T RING, KNOCK!

and picks up his newspaper together with two folded giro slips, he grumbles 'You insatiable bastards!' And we discover that he lives in a round tower.

Through the window the afternoon sunlight falls on the backs of books on their shelves, on an old-fashioned wardrobe and on a wide bed, which is just as he left it in the morning. Louka opens the window to let in some air and in doing so frightens some pigeons. Looking out of the window one would have to agree that the climb was worthwhile. Just as in a spotlit painting by a great master, the centre is held by the baroque dome of St Nicholas's Church with, next to it, like inspired kitsch, the view of Prague Castle.

Louka lies down on the unmade bed, dressed as he is, and reaches for the telephone. He places it on his chest and dials a number.

'That you, Helen darling? This is Louka. I suddenly felt so melancholy and who d'you think I thought of? You, of course. Fact. Would you be too scared to spend a night in a tower? To the theatre? No, I'm not angry, how could I be angry with you? I'll be in touch again. Sure. Hurry up then. So long.'

Louka presses the cradle down and from memory dials another number.

'That you, Susie? This is Louka. I suddenly felt so melancholy and who d'you think I thought of? You, of course. Oh, he's at home? Bye, then.'

The frustrated telephonist hangs up, heaves a sigh and gets up to have something to eat. From his bag he takes two rolls and some ham in aspic. He sits down at the table, switches on the radio which is evidently permanently tuned to Radio Free Europe, props his newspaper against it and eats while he reads.

The voice on the radio is saying something about the days of Communism in Czechoslovakia being numbered. The headline in the paper, on the other hand, asserts that 'Socialism is our ultimate security'. An observant eye would notice that the newspaper page is trembling under the effect of the sound.

Louka removes the wrapping from the litre bottle of red wine, but then changes his mind and does it up again.

He finds the classified ads page and puts on his spectacles to read the small print:

WANTED VW BEETLE – Damaged vehicle considered.
FOR SALE TRABANT 601/77 – in need of attention. Twenty thousand.

'Twenty thousand for one in need of attention – daylight robbery,' Louka grunts in disgust. He takes his trousers off while he is reading and climbs into bed. The small lamp over his head shines on a framed photograph on the wall. It is a group picture captioned 'The Czech Philharmonic Orchestra, 1986'. It shows Louka among the cello players. He is wearing tails, a bow tie and a happy smile.

It is a morning full of birdsong. There isn't a soul about in the cemetery behind the Strašnice Crematorium. Except for one old lady tidying a grave with a little rake.

'Good morning,' Louka's voice disturbs her.

'Good morning,' the widow answers hesitantly, tottering on her feet a little as she gets dizzy straightening up.

'Looking at the lettering – it could do with a little touching up,' says

Louka, pointing to the name Otto Horáček on the tombstone.

'You're right. It's the rain that does it.'

'I do that sort of thing.'

'What do you mean?'

'I renovate inscriptions.'

The woman regards him doubtfully.

'And it doesn't cost much. Five crowns a gold letter, three crowns a silver one,' Louka explains his offer. 'In your case I'd recommend gold because silver wouldn't show up against this stone.'

'No, not silver,' Mrs Horáčková agrees. 'So how much would it come to altogether?'

'You haven't got much here.' Louka traces the letters with his finger.

OTTO HORÁČEK

1905–1979

HERE RESTS IN THE LORD

'That is thirty-eight letters, making one hundred and ninety crowns. But think how beautiful it'll be.'

'Why is it so expensive?' The widow is surprised.

Louka reaches into his satchel and produces a little bottle with gold paint and holds it between the sun and Mrs Horáčková's eyes.

'Because there's real ground gold in it. Do you see those little flakes? Those are gold flakes.'

'Well, it does need it. That's a fact.' The woman, looking at the faded inscription, still hesitates.

'A pity the gentleman spelled his name with two Ts.' Louka points to the Christian name. 'Some Ottos spell it with just one. You'd save a fiver. I tell you what. I'll do the dates for free, that means take away forty, and to hell with the hyphen, so that makes one hundred and forty-five crowns. Is that all right?'

'That's all right,' Mrs Horáčková agrees, relieved. 'And is payment in advance?'

'Not at all. Next time you come to water the flowers you pay it to that young gravedigger there and he'll give it to me.'

With these words Louka pulls out a bluish jacket from his satchel and puts it on.

'First we'll degrease it,' he says and with a rag dipped in some solvent he goes over the letters. 'If your husband were alive I'm sure he'd approve,' he adds inconsequentially.

'Ah yes, you should have known him. He watched every penny, he did,' says the widow, waving her hand at the recollection.

'Franta!' comes a shout from the crematorium building. Louka turns round.

On the path stands Pekárek, the first violin, pantomiming fiddling. Louka nods his head. As he removes his working jacket he reassures the widow: 'Got another job to do. But when you next come here, Mrs Horáčková, you won't recognize the tombstone. All in gold.'

Again they are playing Dvořák and the singer Klára Koutská assumes her place in her high-heeled shoes.

She swallows and then releases her contralto. Although Louka has her attractive behind within his reach and although in the *Biblical Song* there are quite a few bars without the cello, Louka resists the temptation. But what is this? It looks as if Klára is almost imperceptibly moving towards the cello. Louka registers her movement but misses its significance. Except that Klára now actually looks back as if to say: What on earth is the matter with you today? And as she sings she steps back so close to him that it seems a sin not to fondle her behind. But Louka controls himself and commits that sin.

'Christ almighty,' says Klára later in Louka's bed, as they rest together after the tempest. That there was a tempest is confirmed by the state of the floor, which, just as if they were fragments of tiles and ridge-pieces swept from the roof, is scattered with shoes and underwear and outer garments. A half-emptied bottle of red wine testifies that there had been no time for conversation.

'Louka, you chump, do you know how long I've been waiting for this?

Two years,' Klára says with her eyes closed, the purple eye-shadow smudged down to the base of her nose. 'Ever since the funeral of that usherette Hajková from the National Theatre. That was where I first sang with you.'

'That's terrible,' says Louka.

'All this time,' nods Klára, hiccuping.

'It's terrible that we measure time by funerals,' Franta explains his point. 'Just like funeral directors.'

Klára kisses his forehead in a motherly way, smoothes out the wrinkles with her forefinger, and says: 'You were never married, were you?'

'Never. My late father always impressed on me that if you want to achieve anything in music you shouldn't marry. Music is celibacy.'

'Celibacy – no intimacy,' says Klára, hiccuping again.

'Got the hiccups or what?' Louka laughs.

'I always get them when . . . it's been good. Always afterwards.'

Louka takes hold of her hand and advises her: 'Bite your little finger and keep it there. That's where the hiccuping points are.'

Klára presses her little finger between her teeth while Louka continues: 'And later, when I was . . . no longer young I didn't feel like marrying. You're not wanting to get married, I hope?'

'No thanks. I am already,' the singer replies, hiccuping.

'Another good way to stop hiccuping is to let the blood drain out of your left leg and right hand.'

'The left leg and right hand?' Klára asks in surprise and Louka obligingly helps her to point her left leg upwards.

From the window come some strange scratching noises. Klára raises her head. 'What's that?'

'Pigeons. They're sharpening their beaks. On the metal window ledge,' Louka explains.

'Why did they chuck you out of the Philharmonic when you're such a good cellist?' Klára wants to know.

'They banned me from travelling abroad. And such a cellist is useless to a symphony orchestra.'

'Because your brother emigrated?'

'The things you know . . .' says Louka in surprise and nods. 'Because my brother emigrated. But mainly because I'm an idiot. I really don't want to talk about it.'

'And why are they sharpening their beaks?'
asks Klára (Libuše Šafránková), curious about the pigeons.

'Then don't talk about it,' Klára agrees, her leg and arm still sticking up. And as she hasn't hiccuped for some time she's happy it works. 'D'you know it really helps.' Then she returns to the pigeons: 'And why are they sharpening their beaks?'

'That I can explain to you,' says Louka, taking a deep breath as for a detailed explanation. 'To make them sharp.'

'You're an idiot,' says Klára and hiccups.

The inscription on Mr Horáček's tombstone is now nearly all gilt. Only the last two letters are left for Louka to do.

Down the cemetery path comes a green truck. Its driver is Ládík, a lad of eighteen, and next to him, his knees almost touching the windscreen, sits the gravedigger Brož, a man of about thirty-five. The vehicle comes to a stop by the letter painter and Ládík switches off the engine.

'Honour to work.' Brož uses the Communist greeting as he steps out and slams the cab door shut.

'Hello to you,' replies Louka.

'Listen, I have thousands of orders for you.' Brož produces a piece of paper from his pocket. 'Three in gold and two in silver. It's all here. The Roman numerals are the cemetery blocks and the Arabic ones are the graves.'

'That's lovely. A gravedigger like you is a joy to the whole cemetery. Many thanks,' says Louka appreciatively and pushes the paper into his pocket.

'Doesn't he do it well?' Brož turns to Ládík, who has now also climbed down from the truck and shuffled over.

Ládík nods in agreement.

'I'm doing my best. Must be careful not to smudge . . .' says Louka, continuing with his gliding. The two visitors don't seem in any hurry.

'Mr Louka, tell us about that concert in America,' the gravedigger asks after a while.

'Which one's that?'

'That hall you played in.'

'But you've heard that already,' Louka says.

'Young Ládík here hasn't,' says Brož.

14

Louka looks at the youngster with his lanky hair and his goose-like blue eyes. 'Okay. That was in New York. We played *Má Vlast*.'

'By Dvořák, you understand,' Brož explains to Ládík.

'By Smetana,' Louka continues. 'And that Carnegie Hall was bursting at the seams. We didn't get much of a welcome, mind. A sort of lukewarm applause, just polite. We were knackered after the journey, but bit by bit we managed to shake off our exhaustion . . .'

'You forgot to mention those different races . . .' the gravedigger reminds him.

'The races, yes. Well, in that audience were Chinese, Japanese, Mexicans, Blacks. One of them a real giant, so the ones behind him couldn't see . . .'

'Looked like a heavyweight boxer,' Brož adds for Ládík's benefit.

'And I was thinking to myself, what on earth can this mountain of a man with his battered nose and hair like a wire pot-scourer get out of our *Vltava*? Or *Tábor*? He doesn't even know what it is.'

'Now you listen, mate.' Brož nudges Ládík.

'As I said, the fatigue gradually fell from us and we began to play like men possessed. The conductor was sweating till the drops hit us, and when he gave us our attacks *tutti forte* it was like a wet dog shaking itself.'

Ládík, still silent, laughs.

'Don't laugh, you fool. How much weight did you say a conductor loses?' Brož is clearly demanding the full original, complete with marginal notes.

'In the course of a concert a conductor can lose three kilos.' Louka meets his demand. Brož glances at Ládík to gauge his reaction and Ládík nods appreciatively.

'But when we finished playing there was silence. For two or three seconds complete silence. And then it broke loose.'

'The applause, you understand,' Brož quickly interposes for Ládík's benefit.

'Such applause that it gave us a fright. It was like a rock breaking loose and crashing down on us. And as we were standing up to acknowledge it I looked out for the big black guy. And there he was, clapping his great mitts, which were pink on the palms, and tears the size of peas were rolling down his African face. Even though he had no idea that the Vltava is some river in Europe, it was all the same to him because the music had bowled

'Must be careful not to smudge . . .' says Louka, before telling the gravedigger Brož (Ondřej Vetchý) and Ládík (Marek Daniel) about America.

him over. Because music, gentlemen, doesn't care about races or nations. Music doesn't give a damn. There, I have finished,' says Louka, wiping a drip of gold paint from under the final letter and turning to his listeners.

The string quartet is playing *From my Life*. The sounds of the four instruments combine in a rare blend that is unsettling and consoling at the same time. The threads of the music lift us like puppets high above the sun-drenched cemetery.

Shafts of sunlight are piercing the gloom under the ceiling of the crematorium, where the four musicians are weaving that magic tapestry. White rosin falls like snowflakes from the horsehair of Pekárek's bow. Louka's left hand gives the cello a vibrato which lends his clumsy instrument a wistful tenderness. All the musicians are playing with great concentration and one completely forgets that the setting is a funeral parlour.

Forgetting is made even easier by looking at Klára. Women of her age, as is well known, age faster in the face than in the body. Time, which mercilessly works around the eyes and mouth, seems too bashful to get under their clothes and thus leaves many areas unexpectedly girlish. For instance the breasts. As the singer bends over the four mugs to reward the musicians with their coffee, her breasts are almost in their entirety exposed to view.

Klára looks at Louka, who senses it, and their eyes meet for a moment.

The big black bird in the cage says: 'I tell you, lay off! I tell you, lay off!'

Louka watches it with interest. 'What kind of bird is it?' he asks.

'A sacred myna bird,' Brož the gravedigger replies, drawing the cork out of a bottle of Moravian wine. As the bird hears the sound it says: 'Cheers! Cheers!'

'He's a fine talker,' Louka says admiringly.

'Too much of one. Definitely a garrulous bird,' says Brož as he fills a couple of what had been mustard glasses. He comes straight to the point, to the reason why he has invited Louka to his house.

'Your problem with the Trabant could be solved.'

18

'The Trabant perhaps, but what about the money, Mr Brož?'

'Well, that's what it's all about. You've never had a job like this before. Thirty thousand made in a single day. But it's a one-off.' The gravedigger is keeping his guest in suspense while he feeds the fish in his tank with dried ticks.

Louka turns his chair to face the fish tank. But Brož is in no hurry. He lets him watch the mouths of the fish as they swim to the surface for their food before he says at last: 'You're a bachelor, aren't you. At least that's what you said.'

Louka nods.

'Well then, there's an easy thirty thousand within your reach. Just waiting to be swept up.' With a gesture Brož sweeps up an imaginary pile of money off the table.

Brož's two daughters burst into the room. Five-year-old Zuzka carries a puppy in her arms and three-year-old Tanya calls out: 'Daddy! Andy has a tick!'

'And it's full of blood already,' Zuzka says, pointing to a spot under the dog's collar. Brož reaches up to the shelf for some oil. Two cats have slipped into the room behind the girls and rub against Louka's legs. Louka suffers it in silence.

'Have you got an amimal at home?' little Tanya addresses him.

'An animal? No, I haven't.'

'Have you got a child?'

'No child either,' Louka answers under interrogation. It is obvious that conversation with children makes him ill at ease.

'So what have you got?'

Louka shrugs. He would like the confrontation with this strange element to come to an end. 'Go and play outside. I'll see to the tick,' the gravedigger commands his daughters. As the door closes behind them he continues talking while performing twisting motions with his finger on the dog's neck.

'I won't beat about the bush, Mr Louka. It concerns a wedding. We have this old . . . how shall I put it . . . this old aunt.'

'Oh no, Mr Brož. I've no intention of getting married, least of all to an old aunt,' Louka protests.

'Hang on. This aunt is Russian.'

'Worse still, a Russian!'

'We're not talking about the aunt. The aunt has a niece.'

'Not even a niece, Mr Brož.' Louka shakes his head.

'Listen, Mr Louka.' Brož lowers his voice. 'What I'm going to say to you will remain between the two of us. Okay?'

With these words he forces his oily hand on Louka.

'It would be a fictitious marriage.'

'Cheers! Cheers!' the bird interjects.

'He's right. We're forgetting our drinks.' Brož clinks glasses with Louka.

'The niece is over here at her aunt's invitation and she needs our citizenship, you understand. So she doesn't have to return to Russia.'

'The niece?'

'Yes, the niece. By the way, a pretty girl. Now we've got it!' Brož has at last freed the tick and regards the blob on his finger with disgust. He tears off a piece of newspaper, puts a match to it in an ashtray, and as he flicks the parasite into the flame he remarks: 'We have burial by cremation in these parts, you parasite.'

He immediately continues: 'Six months later you get a divorce and you're free as a bird again.'

There is the trilling sound of the telephone ringing. Brož takes no notice, even though the instrument is right by his hand. He is waiting for Louka's answer. When it rings again Louka glances at the instrument.

'The phone.'

'No, that's him.' The gravedigger points to the cage. 'He imitates everything. If he didn't shit up the whole place he'd be quite an intelligent creature. Just look at it.' Brož points to the bird droppings around the cage. There are even some droppings on the back of his jacket.

'What age do they live to?' asks Louka, anxious to get the conversation away from Brož's crazy idea.

'Thirty in the wild, twenty in captivity.'

'There you are, and you want me to get married.' Louka himself reverts to the subject. 'We live longer when we're free. In captivity we're soon done for.'

Mrs Brož enters the kitchen. On her lap, which betrays an advanced state of pregnancy, she is carrying another puppy.

'Is Andy here?'

'Sure. He had a tick.' Brož releases Andy from his lap.

'Phew, I was worried he'd run away. Good morning.'

Mrs Brož would have clearly liked to meet the guest, but the gravedigger was in no mood for this.

'Leave us alone, Maruš. We're talking business,' he says.

'Oh. Come here, you bundle of trouble. I already pictured you under the wheels of some car or other.' The gravedigger's wife lovingly places Andy on the ledge of her belly. Before leaving the room she says: 'You know what I think of it.'

'Calm down, Maruš. Don't worry.'

'A fictitious wedding, Mr Louka. Only pretend. For forty grand!' Brož continues as the door closes.

'You said thirty,' Louka corrects him.

'She would go to forty if it came to it. A Trabant station wagon plus I'd write off twenty thousand from what you owe me. Seems to me a better deal than gilding graves,' says Brož.

'Graves! Always graves! Bloody job!' the sacred myna bird calls out. A moment later there comes some thumping from the floor.

Surprised, Louka looks under the table and sees a rabbit. 'You've got a lot of animals, I see,' he says.

'You've got to when you're a gravedigger. Have living creatures around, I mean. Her name's Nadezhda and it would be a mere formality. So what do you think, Mr Louka?'

'No go, Mr Brož,' says Louka. 'That's not my cup of tea, really. Not my kind of thing at all.'

The express train thunders past and the airstream bends the stems of the weeds growing alongside the track.

František Louka has a window seat and reads a newspaper. As he is looking at the back page we can see the front-page headlines:

Perestroyka concerns us all

The impossible becomes reality

Satire is a frail flower.

G 52923 LIMERICK COUNTY LIBRARY

Louka rubs his eyes, drops the paper on his lap and watches the landscape slip by.

Louka, his cello in one hand and a suitcase in the other, is walking through his home town. Low buildings alternate with two-storey houses. He exchanges greetings with a cyclist and then with a postwoman.

'Come to see your mother, have you?' The postwoman smiles.

'That's right,' Louka agrees.

The brand new building of the Party secretariat has two Tatra-613s parked in front.

'Seen anything like it, Franta?' a disabled man in a wheelchair hails him.

'Hi, Honza, how goes it?' Louka asks.

'It's going downhill. Know what they call this building? They call it the coconut.' The man in the wheelchair has lowered his voice.

'Coconut?'

'Yeah, the Communist council nuthouse.' Honza utters a smoker's guffaw, which turns into such a violent cough that Louka has to hit his back to prevent him from choking.

'Visiting your mother?' The old man cheerfully wipes off his tears.

'Just so,' Louka replies.

He crosses the square, where red tulips are planted in the shape of a five-pointed star. At the centre of it Lenin on a plinth sticks up his chin towards the sky as if he were sunbathing.

From the public address system of the local radio comes march music, followed by a female voice re-echoing from the more distant streets:

'Attention all rabbit breeders. Because of the prevalence of myxomatosis there is a need to immunize your animals. Detailed information from Comrade Bílý, chairman of the Small Animals Breeders' Association.

'We also wish to invite all lovers of classical music to a concert of works by the composer Vivaldi in the town hall at eight p.m. today. The performers are František Louka, violoncello, and students from the Janáček Music Academy in Brno. Admission fifteen crowns.'

By now Louka has reached the family home and opens the garden gate.

The heavy front door of the villa, with its paint curled into lichen-like patterns by the sun, closes behind Louka with a grating sound, shutting out the march music which followed the public announcement.

Inside a piano is heard. It is the playing of a pupil, with frequent stops and resumptions from where a mistake was made.

Louka leans his cello against the wall on which hangs an old poster. It shows a students' string quintet. The clean-shaven youngster behind the cello is obviously Louka.

The visitor, his presence still unnoticed, lets his eyes dwell on the objects in his home. There is an ugly flower stand: the top flower-pots contain a spider plant that trails down to some cacti. There is an embroidered picture of a blue stream running through a white countryside, with a footbridge. Then there are two sacred scenes painted on birchwood, in which an unknown artist has copied some coloured picture postcards of the Sacred Hill and the Sacred Mountain. Leaning against the corner is a stick adorned with little shields of castles visited.

Louka hangs his coat on a brass hook by the mirror which is tarnished with age and which distorts. He bends his knees to see if the uneven surface still deforms his face as it did, to his amusement, in his childhood. Without knocking he enters the room.

A little girl of six, sitting at the piano, sees him first and stops playing. Only then does his mother turn round.

'Frankie,' she exclaims, her voice full of emotion. With one hand on the piano and the other on the shoulder of her pupil, the old lady gets up and embraces her son.

'You took the eleven o'clock, that's wonderful! I thought you'd be taking the three p.m. Maruška, we'll stop for today. Practise this piece at home and come back on Tuesday. But lots of practising, mind. Today was really terrible.'

While Maruška picks up her music and leaves with a soft 'Good-bye', the old lady makes for the kitchen, chattering gaily.

'I felt you might come. Do you know what I've made for lunch? Miners' stew! I was telling them at the pharmacy: "Frankie is coming, so I'll make miners' stew." '

'That's perfect,' says Louka, looking around to see what is new in the room.

Besides the piano there is a massive wing armchair and some solid nineteen-thirties furniture. On the walls are some oil paintings: a Czech landscape, a stormy sea and a still-life with flowers. There is also a painting entitled 'The Apostles of the Czech Language', depicting the nation's great men from different centuries, all swearing an oath to protect their language. On top of the bookcase are three small plaster busts: Masaryk, Beneš and Štefánik.

Behind the glass of the bookcase Louka notices an envelope with foreign stamps. He takes it out.

'A letter from Vic. It came yesterday. He's sent some lovely photographs.'

Louka inspects the lovely photographs. They show his brother, his sister-in-law and their ten-year-old son. They are laughing in front of an open fireplace; they are laughing over a birthday cake; they are laughing in the garden, and by their car. The colours are all brighter than natural and they are all suntanned.

'And you haven't even sent a postcard. The Philharmonic was in Belgium. Weren't you with them? I know it all from the radio. And you can't even drop a line to your old mother. Vic writes every other week,' Louka's mother reproaches him over her cooking.

'There wasn't any time, Mum. The Belgians were driving us like a herd of goats,' Louka lies.

'He writes a good letter. He's rented new premises for his surgery. Read it aloud if you're reading it,' the old lady demands.

Louka replaces the letter and the photographs in the envelope.

'I'm not reading it. Maybe later, Mum,' he says.

Mother and son eat their miners' stew. Potatoes and dumplings, with fried onion scattered on top.

'Sometimes I think you don't like Vic,' his mother says. 'What's he done to you? He's your brother, after all.'

'What he's done to me is that he ran away.'

'So what? You can't hold that against him. He went there with no more than the clothes on his back and now he has a good practice.'

'He has a good practice and I have bugger-all.'

'You'll be making money again, Frankie. As a virtuoso you'll do well again.' The old woman strokes her son's beard with a wrinkled and brown-spotted hand. 'I'm curious to see how many will come tonight. Oh yes, Frankie, Mr Holeček said we ought to renew the guttering,' the mother says between mouthfuls. Louka stops chewing.

'New guttering?'

'He says it's rusted through. The rainwater gets under the rendering. He says that two thousand would do it. Material and labour.'

Louka puts his knife and fork down: 'For heaven's sake, Mum, where would I find that kind of money? Don't you know I've been skint on account of this house? I sold my car, I sank all my savings into it. Where would I find the money?'

'How can you talk like this, Frankie?' says the old lady in amazement. The fork in her hand trembles with excitement. 'This house belongs to you now that you've bought Vic's half-share. Otherwise they'd have confiscated it because of Vic's being an emigrant. Would you have wanted that? For me to live here with strangers?'

'Not now when we're eating . . .' And Louka turns to his plate again.

Louka has changed into a pair of old corduroys and a torn jumper and has climbed a ladder to the guttering. The channel is blocked by mud and broken tiles; grass is sprouting in several places, there is even a birch sapling there. Louka clears the debris with a trowel and shovels it into a bucket.

'Don't fall down, Frankie. You've got a concert tonight,' Mrs Louka calls from below.

A man around forty is walking along the pavement, carrying a case. He is Louka's friend Houdek. He calls out: 'Hi, Franta! Still playing to the corpses?'

His mother clearly does not understand the question.

Louka changes his footing on the ladder in embarrassment and tries to avoid an answer.

'What about you? Still blowing the reeds for the gall-bladder patients?'

'Sure. A spa orchestra, what else? Don't you want to join us? We play cheerful pieces. Got a train to catch. So long, then. Good-bye, Mrs Louka.'

Mrs Louka's eyes follow him suspiciously. 'What is he suggesting? A concert virtuoso like you playing on some colonnade? And what did he mean by those corpses?'

'That's what we call a concert audience when it is dead. When it's not responding. It was blocked here, this whole channel. Otherwise the

'Looks like costume jewellery. Sort of trinket you'd buy at a fair,' says his mother (Stella Zázvorková), doubting the value of Louka's find.

guttering is still fairly okay,' Louka assures her, even though his trowel has just gone right through the metal.

Something glistens in the black mud. Louka frees the object from a tangle of small roots and wipes it on his sweater. It seems strange, but there is no mistake. He is holding a jewel of some kind in his hand. A piece of ladies' jewellery with small cut stones.

'Well, I'm damned. How did this thing get up here? Can't have fallen from the sky.' Louka climbs down to his mother.

'This was up there?' She puts on her spectacles.

'Yes.'

'But this isn't worth much, Frankie. Looks like costume jewellery. Sort of trinket you'd buy at a fair.' She hands him back his find.

'You can't be sure. But tell me, how did it get up there?' Louka cleans the trinket in the water butt and it sparkles in the sun.

The quintet that is playing Vivaldi in the hall of the National Committee is made up of young musicians. Louka belongs to their fathers' generation and he has to work hard to keep up with them. The youngsters are taming the demanding work like a beautiful stallion whose antics they are familiar with. They know the places where he could throw them and they are watching out for them. And when they overcome them they feel happy in their saddles and continue with joyful fervour; Louka winks at them to show how he enjoys riding along with them.

It is a pity that there are only six or seven people in the audience, most of them elderly. The most affected of them is Louka's mother. She has eyes only for her son. Small wonder that she is furious with the neighbour on her left, who, in spite of the brilliant performance, has fallen asleep and is now disturbing it by his snoring.

'Please, Mr Šourek!' she says, elbowing him angrily.

The thin applause of twelve palms dies down and the musicians pack up their instruments in the storeroom behind the hall, which serves also as a depository of flags and banners for International Women's Day, the anniversary of the Great October Revolution and May Day.

'I'm sorry, gentlemen, the people are hopeless. We had posters out, I announced it over the local radio, and we have an empty hall,' laments Mrs

Beránková, the official in charge of culture.

'We are used to outnumbering our audience. But we gave a fine performance, didn't we?' A student with a viola accepts the situation in good humour.

'A fine performance, boys, a fine performance. A real joy,' Louka agrees.

'Except what about money, Mr Louka? We'll pay the young people's travel expenses, of course, but all I've collected is ninety crowns and I feel really embarrassed vis-à-vis you, Mr Louka . . .'

'Take it as a voluntary contribution, Mrs Beránková. To show my love for the town,' Louka reassured the unhappy official.

'You really don't mind?'

'Cross my heart,' lies Louka.

In the door stands old Mrs Louka with her shield-decorated walking stick.

'A wonderful experience, gentlemen! A musical treat. Beyond what money can buy.'

'Unfortunately,' says Louka and makes the students laugh.

In an antique shop on Národní Street an expert's bulging eye examines the jewel.

'Where did you get this?'

'I found it,' Louka replies.

'Found it . . .' grunts the expert and reaches for a more powerful magnifying glass.

'And what do you think it's worth?' The dealer increases the suspense.

'That's what I want you to tell me.'

'I could offer you . . . five, perhaps ten crowns.' With a wry smile the man hands the trinket back to Louka.

'Crowns?' Louka double-checks and leaves the shop, disappointed.

'Only explanation is a chimney-sweep,' says the first violinist, inspecting the mysterious piece of costume jewellery over a pair of frankfurters and mustard in the interval between two funerals. 'Bought it for his wife, swept a chimney and it fell out of his pocket.'

'At our place the chimney-sweep doesn't climb up on the roof. Only sweeps it from below.' Louka rejects the solution. He adds: 'Jardo, I know I haven't repaid you that hundred-crown note, but could you lend me another?'

The organist, who is in charge in the loft of the Strašnice Crematorium, picks up the telephone on the desk by the organ.

'*Golden Sunshine*, good, we haven't done that for a while, and *The Old Mother* as a conclusion. The customer's always right.' He calls his colleagues back to work.

'Enough, gentlemen. Shine upon me, golden sunshine!'

The musicians sit down at their desks.

Brož the gravedigger has a different theory.

'Couple walking down the street. Your street. They're arguing. She says: "You can go to hell and so can the trinket you gave me." Takes it off and furiously chucks it right into your guttering. That's how I see it.'

Louka, intent on the letters he is painting, this time in silver, replies: 'I agree, Mr Brož.'

'Quite so. Because there's no other explanation.' Brož is about to leave.

'That idea of yours, about that sham wedding – I mean I agree to it,' Louka explains.

Through the sleepy and bored eyes of the waiter we observe a small group of people sitting around a formica-topped table in an unpretentious restaurant on the Spořilov estate. Louka and Brož have cups of coffee in front of them, the elderly stout aunt Tamara and her niece Nadezhda, a thirty-three-year-old brunette, are drinking tea.

In order to see the fifth guest, for whom the yellow lemonade is evidently intended, we'd have to look lower down. Kneeling on the floor is a five-year-old boy. Using his chair as a table, he is drawing something with coloured crayons.

Brož and aunt Tamara, who is rolling one cigarette after another, have already filled the ashtray with a pile of stubs, testifying to protracted and difficult negotiations. As we are approaching the group the waiter has just changed the ashtray by the professional trick of first covering the full ashtray with an empty one.

'If you know speak in German, you speak with Nadezhda in German, because she interpreter from in Russian language to in German,' aunt Tamara explains in broken Czech, pronouncing the Czech words as if they were Russian.

'I don't know either German or Russian, unfortunately.' Louka shrugs.

'Clear to me. You first disliking Germans and then disliking Russians.' Aunt Tamara understandingly slaps Louka's back and then translates for Nadezhda.

'Nothing to do with dislike. I just haven't got a head for languages,' Louka explains.

'But that's neither here nor there,' says Brož, entering the debate. 'Nobody's going to be interested how you two talk together. Every Czech knows a little Russian . . .'

When he sees that Nadezhda doesn't understand, he repeats in Russian: 'Every Czech knows a little Russian.'

'Except me,' says Louka.

'Except Mr Louka here every Czech knows a little Russian.' The gravedigger has at last arrived at a final definition.

'Except him?' Nadezhda asks in surprise, having understood the last bit.

'But nobody will find this suspicious.' Brož turns to Tamara. 'The important thing is that Maestro Louka here knows that everything is above board. No tricks. A divorce within six months and that's it.'

'I you promise that's it, Mr Maestro,' says aunt Tamara, striking her breast. 'Fiction marriage. For appearance marriage. We nothing hide: Nadezhda a little son has; you seen him. She young, you could her father be. How she have interest in you? What with you would she do?'

Louka looks at his future bride and wryly nods in agreement. Nadezhda, not knowing what her aunt has said, smiles at him. Then she remembers something: 'Tamara, tell him that everything is to be just like a real wedding,' Nadezhda says in Russian.

The aunt translates into her broken Czech: 'Nadezhda says everything to be like real wedding. Because police can watch. Fiction weddings now often made, and police not stupid. Therefore everything like real wedding. Wedding reception and first night.'

'What first night?' Louka turns questioningly to Brož.

'Got to spend the wedding night together. Each one in their own room. Just so you don't attract attention by each of you going off in a different direction,' the gravedigger reassures him.

'Waiter, I'll have a cognac,' says Louka.

From under the table comes a growl as the little boy imitates the sound of the car he has just drawn. He stops and watches a small package travelling from aunt Tamara's knees to Brož's knees and on to another pair of knees.

'Deposit,' whispers Brož, almost without opening his mouth, and furtively places the envelope on Louka's lap.

When Louka has put it away in his pocket aunt Tamara leans over to him confidentially: 'Do you know how much it cost to bribe the Russian officials?'

Louka shakes his head: he doesn't know.

The aunt pulls him even closer by his sleeve and says: 'Don't ask.'

The red carpet of the Vyšehrad hall for wedding ceremonies, that bridge which thousands of couples have crossed into the state of matrimony, has on its left side a path for men that is perceptible only to the attentive eye, whereas the right half is visibly holed by the stiletto heels of the brides. Today this fateful carpet muffles the uncertain step of the polished black brogues of František Louka and the somewhat bolder tread of Nadezhda Ivanovna Bilyukova's white shoes.

The organ plays Brahms and Mendelssohn; the official reads from the tablets of wisdom about the beautiful bond between man and woman; the photographer takes his pictures, and the couple nod and say yes. There are only two wedding guests – aunt Tamara and the little boy. He holds on to her hand and with serious eyes watches the unfamiliar theatre before him. He is interested in the strange animal in the national coat-of-arms, in the organist, the photographer and the fretwork back of the antique chair.

One slight hiccup occurs nevertheless. While the first ring is smoothly slipped on the bride's finger, the second, try as they might, doesn't get past Louka's thick knuckle.

Louka's mouldy beard approaches the young lips.

The groom signs in Latin script, the bride in Cyrillic. The signatures of the witnesses follow suit, because Louka's witness is the gravedigger Brož and Nadezhda's her Russian girlfriend Pasha, a woman with big gold earrings and front teeth of the same metal.

As Pasha signs her name she turns and gives Kolya a cheerful toothy smile.

Louka is made nervous not only by the ceremony itself, which he had successfully avoided all his life, but mainly by the organist who is staring at him incessantly over his horn-rimmed glasses, as if he can't believe his eyes. Now he has even exchanged his reading glasses for his distant-vision ones, having first breathed on them and wiped the lenses on the lapel of his jacket, to make absolutely sure his eyes do not deceive him. Louka bows his head, but in vain. Coincidence is an ass: the organist today is his colleague Musil. When the ceremony finishes and the witnesses together with aunt Tamara congratulate the newly married couple, Musil cannot resist and joins them.

'Well, Franta, I'm amazed. Best of luck! A beauty! A real beauty!' he says, winking stupidly at Louka.

'You'd just have to play everywhere, wouldn't you?' the bridegroom sourly thanks him. And this is the only dialogue of this otherwise mute and organ-accompanied spectacle.

The wedding party are quietly lunching in a small private room in a restaurant. All that can be heard is the tinkle of soup spoons against the bowls. Only the gravedigger Brož ruffles the monotonous sound backdrop by his slurping.

'Borshch like with us,' says aunt Tamara.

'Very tasty,' agrees Pasha in Russian.

'*Da*,' says the bride, eating out of a common bowl with her husband.

And again only clatter and slurping.

The five-year-old boy is sitting beside aunt Tamara. He is bored.

He doesn't like the soup.

'A beauty! A real beauty!' says Musil (Karel Heřmánek), winking stupidly at Louka through his spectacles.

'Eat up, eat up,' Tamara urges him in Russian, but the boy refuses. He puts his head in her lap. The elderly woman strokes his hair and then reaches under the table for her handbag.

'Nadezhda not like to hear it,' she says to Louka, 'but never have time for Kolya. She study, she interpret, all international conferences, and who bring up boy?'

The aunt has at last found a photo in her handbag.

'Know who this is?'

'You?' guesses Louka, because the face of the elderly woman in the snapshot is quite a bit like Tamara.

'My sister. Mother of Nadezhda. Granny of Kolya. Year ago she die. In town Novosibirsk. She bring him up. And when Kolya brought over here, I for him became *babushka*. Granny Tamara. Kolya, little treasure . . .'

'This is boring for him, isn't it?' says Brož. 'We'll take him to our house. There he'll have dogs, children, a bird, everything.'

Louka isn't interested in the domestic arrangements of this strange family and it embarrasses him that the aunt is initiating him into them as if he were a real husband. When the newly weds' soup plate is empty he excuses himself for a moment.

But he isn't going to the toilet. After a brief conversation with the waiter he is taken to the kitchen, where there's a telephone by the sink. A girl dishwasher, her face flushed, is coping with a mountain of greasy crockery with a song on her lips.

'Mr Musil, please. He plays the organ at your place,' Louka says into the receiver.

'They're on their way, they're on their way, the deer upon the mountains,' the dishwasher sings while he waits.

'Hi, Eman, this is Louka. Yes, Franta.' He sticks a finger into his other ear to shut out the deer. 'Eman, please, don't breathe a word about this to anyone. Understand? What? Good party? Yes, a good party. Just a moment . . .' He covers the receiver with his hand and asks the singing woman: 'Could you please sing less loud?'

The woman stops altogether, so that Louka's voice can now be heard throughout the kitchen.

'Yes, I want you to keep what you saw at Vyšehrad strictly under your hat. In other words, don't breathe a word about that wedding to anyone. I'll explain to you later. Yes, I got married, but I don't want it to be known.'

The dishwasher laughs aloud at this and so does the chef.

'By all means sing, but not so loud,' says Louka, covering the receiver's mouthpiece.

'Either I sing properly or I don't sing at all.' The singer rejects the compromise offered. And so Louka concludes his conversation not only for Musil but for a suddenly hushed kitchen:

'Just keep your mouth shut about it. I'll explain everything later. What? You've already told whom? You are an idiot, Eman.' Louka, utterly crushed, slams down the receiver.

'And with his finger on the trigger the huntsman cuts a splendid figure . . .' the mischievously cheerful voice of the dishwasher accompanies his exit from the kitchen.

Two taxis convey the wedding party across Prague to the Spořilov estate. Brož is sitting next to the first driver. Louka is sitting in the back, next to his bride, and despondently stares out of the window. The second taxi carries aunt Tamara and the witness Pasha. Now and again the aunt looks back, perhaps out of fear that the sham wedding is being observed by someone.

On the table in Tamara's living room stands a big samovar. From a tape recorder comes the voice of a Russian tenor, accompanied by balalaikas. The party is in full swing, carrying Louka up to heights from which he must soon fall. A Soviet champagne cork narrowly misses the Czech cut-glass chandelier, bounces off the ceiling, hits the icon on the wall and comes to a halt on the worn Persian carpet. Brož picks it up and places it on the table next to its two elder brothers who have swollen from their sudden freedom. The drink fizzes in the glasses and the five people united by this strange wedding clink them and drain them to the bottom. Aunt Tamara is rolling a cigarette and softly singing in unison with the tenor on the tape recorder. Nadezhda's girlfriend keeps topping up Louka's glass, leaning close to him and smiling at him with her gold incisors. Then she playfully pulls his beard and whispers something in Tamara's ear. This

'One wedding is enough. Don't want another,' says Louka.

makes the aunt laugh and she immediately translates for the bridegroom: 'Frank, Pasha here say you handsome man. When you divorced and free again, she like to marry you.' Everybody laughs, except Louka.

'One wedding is enough. Quite enough. Don't want another,' he says, gazing with emotion at his bride.

'You're in demand, Mr Louka,' laughs Brož. 'If you like you can have a re-run. Pasha's a pretty girl too. All that gold . . .'

'Friends.' Louka suddenly decides to make a speech.

'*Druzya*,' the aunt translates, exhaling a cloud of exhaust gases from her smoke-filled lungs.

'I like my wife very much.'

The aunt translates into Russian.

'And I have just decided . . .'

Aunt Tamara continues to translate, expecting some joke.

'. . . that the two of us, that is I and my wife Nadezhda, are today going to spend a real and beautiful, a really beautiful, wedding night.'

Brož, who has just swallowed a piece of *piroshka*, chokes on it. Aunt Tamara stops smiling and stops translating. But the two Russian girls are curious.

'What did he say?' asks Goldieteeth and Nadezhda's dark-brown eyes are also full of questions.

'Just a joke,' says the aunt and stubs her cigarette.

'Because it would be a great pity if,' continues Louka, warmed up by his subject, 'since we now belong to each other . . .' (Here he points to his ring which is still stuck on his finger-joint) '. . . if a Czech man were to deny his beautiful Russian wife her inalable . . . inalienable right.'

At these words he strokes his bride's thick Siberian hair.

'Tamara, translate, translate!' demands the bride.

But aunt Tamara shakes her head.

The telephone rings. Nadezhda, almost as if she'd expected a call, jumps up and runs to it.

'František, you have drunk much.' The aunt turns to him in a motherly fashion.

'We have all drunk much,' Louka replies. He tries to refill his glass but is prevented by Brož who whispers something in his ear.

Meanwhile Nadezhda is talking German to somebody, and very warmly at that. Only a few words can be caught through the general hubbub: '*Ja,*

Gert, ja. Ich auch ... Wann? In Oktober? Wunderbar ... Ich glaube ... Er ist nicht da, aber ... Geschenk? Wirklich? Ich weiss nicht ... Danke, Gert, danke ...'

But Louka is not to be shaken. 'And because we have drunk a lot I now ask the guests to depart to their various homes, Brož for example, and leave the newly weds alone. Because a wedding night, friends, is something unique. We should realize that. And I want my wife Nadezhda to have an unfor ... unforgettable memory of Prague. So that, when she sits wrapped in her fur by her fire in Siberia, she can tell everyone that Czech men are supermen to an advanced age. And I promise that this night I shall be a real Ilya Muromets!'

By now only Pasha is listening to Louka. Nadezhda has finished talking on the phone and aunt Tamara has managed to acquaint her with her bridegroom's unexpected intentions. She is now consulting Brož about what to do.

'Ilya Muromets!' Pasha, recognizing the name of the legendary Russian hero, claps her hands and draws Louka to her by his beard in order to kiss him.

'Or Churila Plenkovich!' adds Louka, remembering the name of another hero of Russian legend.

'Mr Louka, these people don't know you. They don't know you're just joking and they're quite terrified.' Brož tries to pacify Louka, but Louka resists:

'That's quite in order. Every bride is terrified before her wedding night.' Just then a bell rings.

Brož goes to the door and sees his pregnant wife Maruška. She is out of breath and looks worried. With one hand she supports her heavy belly and the other holds the hand of the crying Kolya.

'I think it's time, Joe. The contractions are coming regularly,' she says hurriedly. Looking down to her left she adds: 'He doesn't want to be with us. Cries all the time. You must get back to the children.'

Kolya has meanwhile slipped inside, bypassing Brož, seeking shelter first in Tamara's lap and then with his mother. The women are stroking him and soothing him with whining Russian words. For good measure Goldie-teeth joins them.

'Maruš's time's come. Taxi's waiting, so we're off.' Brož cuts them short while slipping on his coat.

When Tamara translates this, the three women's laments switch from Kolya to Maruška. They stroke her, reassure her and urge her to hurry. Louka is left alone at the table, feeling superfluous. He raises his glass for a toast, he wants to introduce his bride to Mrs Brož, but nobody takes any notice of him.

The Brožes leave and silence descends on the flat.

Only Nadezhda's and Pasha's quiet voices are heard from the next room as they settle the child down in his bed. Aunt Tamara is rolling a cigarette. When she has lit it she points to a sofa with a byzantine rug and in a husky smoker's voice says: 'You'll sleep here.'

It sounds like a verdict.

The aunt opens a chest of drawers and pulls out a man's nightshirt. She flings it on the sofa and says: 'Is clean. From my husband.'

Louka, as if suddenly sobered up, obediently begins to undress. From the next room the aunt brings in an eiderdown and wishes him good night.

Louka lies in the darkened room. Outside, dawn is breaking and the first birds are awakening.

'Nadezhda Ivanovna, my wife!' the unhappy husband calls out weakly.

As if in reply comes the sound of a key being turned in the door behind which the bride sleeps.

Louka's tired eyes stray about the room for a little longer.

The samovar tap is dripping. His jacket is hanging over the back of a chair. Louka reaches into its breast pocket and pulls out a fat envelope with banknotes. With this envelope on his chest he falls asleep.

A freshly washed Trabant hatchback is happily bowling along the motorway, leaving behind it clouds of two-stroke exhaust fumes. What makes it gleam even more is the load it carries on its roof-rack, held down by a spider of bunjee cords – brand-new guttering and downpipes. It is some time since Louka last drove, so he watches the road carefully and accustoms himself to the unfamiliar gear change. He flicks out his right blinker, the car exits from the motorway and is soon travelling along a tarmacked road lined by old trees whose overhanging branches have turned the road into a tunnel.

As he unties the zinc guttering in front of his mother's house and carries it into the garden, a convoy of Soviet army vehicles rumbles down the street. His mother, leaning on a stick, has come out to look at her son's car. She has to shout to make herself heard over the noise of the truck engines.

'New, is it?'

'By no means new, Mum,' Louka replies.

'No? Looks almost new to me. No rust anywhere.'

'These cars don't rust, Mum.'

'They don't? Got a good buy then.'

Looking at the military convoy she remarks spitefully: 'Look, how many of them there are! Like locusts!'

Inside, over his favourite miners' stew, his mother continues: 'Would you believe that a lot of our people are doing deals with them. Buying cheap diesel from them, and petrol, and coal . . . Hand in glove with those occupiers, a fine lot of patriots! When they moved in they raised their fists, swore they'd give them no water and no bread – and now look at them.'

The windows are rattling with the roar of the heavy engines. Even the little busts of forbidden Czech statesmen are trembling on the bookcase.

'You wouldn't believe,' the old lady addresses them, 'the kind of nation we've become. Good thing you didn't live to see it.'

'I've brought you some chocolate and coffee.' From his briefcase Louka produces some western goods and places them by his mother.

'You played abroad? Where was that? Must have missed it,' old Mrs Louka says in surprise.

'We were . . .' Louka casts a quick glance at the chocolate wrapping to discover its origin '. . . in Switzerland.'

'The Swiss always made the best chocolate,' his mother says and, out of context, asks: 'Would you believe that a Czech girl could marry a Russian? The Nováček girl, the ones by the station, got married to a Russian officer. Would you believe it?'

Frank, his mouth full, shakes his head at this decline of morals.

The scene that follows might have been marked by a composer *Allegro molto*, or very fast.

The Trabant is weaving through Prague's heavy traffic.

In the back it carries a cello.

Outside the gate of the Motoly Crematorium Louka takes his instrument out of the hatch and hurries with it to the funeral.

He enters the building by the side door. Soon one can hear the fast final chords of the piece, and already Louka, his case on his back, is striding down the hill to his car.

Another adroit drive through Prague. Louka overtakes Volvos and Mercedeses. In Pavlov Square he takes advantage of the traffic cop just explaining something to a stranger with a map and shoots through the red light just in front of the noses of the cars which have just started from his left. The cop looks up, blows his whistle and is about to take down his number, but Louka's Trabant has filled the intersection with thick smoke.

Just as he overtook all the cars, so now in the forecourt of the Strašnice Crematorium he overtakes the mourners. He actually knocks a wreath from the hands of one of them.

Up the spiral staircase Louka's legs race to the organ loft. All we see during the accelerated play of the quartet is a pair of feet under the cello bow slipping out of their shoes and then slipping them on again. And once more those feet are tripping down the stairs.

Louka has just loaded his cello into the Trabant when he spots Klára. The singer either doesn't see him or pretends not to see him. She focuses her eyes on the number of the tram that is just pulling up at the Crematorium stop.

'Can I give you a lift?' Louka offers.

Klára hesitates for a moment and then gets in.

For a while they drive in silence.

'A wedding present?' Klára says suddenly and blinks – the way women do when their eyes fill with tears.

Louka is caught by surprise. 'That man Musil blabs wherever he goes,' he sighs.

'Nice car. You're going up in the world. In every respect.'

Louka doesn't know what to say. 'Look, Klára, that whole wedding . . .'

'I don't want to know.' Klára cuts him short.

'Let me explain!'

'I really am not interested. It's all pointless now.'

'But I still live on my own. Nothing's changed.'

'For me everything's changed. Everything,' Klára sobs into her handkerchief. 'I'm such a fool. I nearly got divorced because of you.'

At that moment Louka makes a rather unfortunate suggestion: 'Come to the tower with me.'

Thereupon his lover puts her handkerchief back in her handbag and says: 'Stop here. I'm getting out.'

'Klára, dear . . .' Louka begs, reaching for her hand.

'I should like to get out,' says Klára distantly.

The driver stops and a few seconds later looks at her pretty legs receding before moving off.

Carrying a bag with some food and with his instrument on his back Louka conquers the stairs up to his tower. He meets his neighbour, who is briskly running down.

'Coming from a concert?' he hollers as always. 'Successful?'

'Terrific. Not a single dry eye in the house,' Louka replies.

'Changing my exhaust,' the neighbour boasts.

'By yourself?'

'Sure. I do everything myself.'

On the floor below his a door opens and Mrs Buštíková, a woman of about sixty-five, blocks his way with an armful of washing.

'Heard you come up. It's all washed and ironed.'

'Great,' says Louka, taking the pile of washing from her.

'Listen, Mr Louka. One's supposed to decorate one's windows. So you'll put some little flags up, won't you?' says Mrs Buštíková.

'Another anniversary? I can't keep up with them,' Louka says in astonishment.

'Victorious February, Mr Louka. And they're going to note down who's got flags out and who hasn't. Better put something up.'

'But my windows are so high up you can't see them from the street anyway,' Louka objects.

'Don't you believe it. They're watching it like hawks. Also darned a pair of socks for you. They had holes in the heel and in the foot. You don't by any chance walk about in your socks? Listen, you put up one Russian flag and one of ours, so I don't have any aggro from the street committee. You owe me seventy for today's lot; that includes the darning. I'll just add it to the two hundred you owe me already.'

'I'll pay you now,' says Louka, leaning his cello against the wall and pulling out his purse.

'Now?' The woman is surprised.

'Why not.' Louka hands her three one-hundred notes.

'But I've got no change . . .'

'Forget it.' Louka further shocks the already gobsmacked washerwoman, picks up his instrument and continues the climb to his flat.

'Hello,' suddenly comes a voice from above.

Sitting on the last step is a girl of about eighteen.

As she gets up and straightens her skirt, Louka observes in the dim light on the landing that she has long legs and long hair. Behind her, leaning against the wall, is a cello in a canvas cover.

'Hello to you,' he says pleasantly.

'Mr Stoklasa sent me.'

'Stoklasa. Oh,' Louka says, putting his cello next to the girl's. 'Would you mind holding my washing?'

With his hands thus freed Louka starts to unlock his door. In doing so he brushes against his instrument, which slips down until the necks of the two cellos are crossed.

'Not so fast, not so fast,' Louka shouts at his forward instrument and removes it. 'And what has Mr Stoklasa to say to me?' he asks, having steered his unexpected visitor inside.

'You should look me over. Or rather, listen to me,' the girl answers with a smile. In the full light now Louka can see that she is beautiful. Her hair is like a mane and her breasts under a black blouse boldly announce that they are bra-free.

'So you're going to decorate your windows for the anniversary . . .' the girl says, looking about the room with the unmade bed.

'Don't bet on it! I've grown out of that,' says Louka. 'How long have you been playing? Can I offer you a drink?'

'Not very long. A drink would be fine.' The girl answers both questions.

Louka pours a glass of red wine for her from the started bottle.

'I play the viola, but I want to learn the cello,' says the girl after taking a generous sip.

'And what . . .'

'Blanka, is your reason?' the long-haired girl wittily introduces herself, and immediately continues: 'What I like is that it's so big.'

'You like big instruments then?'

'Yes.'

Louka unbuttons his collar.

'Okay, play something.'

Blanka unsheathes her instrument while Louka watches her. He pours himself another glass. Blanka sits down and tightens her bow. Louka takes her hand in his. 'You've got long fingers. That's good.'

The inspection of Blanka's hand takes longer than is necessary to establish the length of her fingers. 'Go ahead, play.'

'You're making me a little nervous,' the girl says by the way of preface. She blows her hair out of her eyes and begins to play.

'Hold it tighter between your legs,' Louka interrupts after a few strokes of the bow, putting his hands on her knees.

The girl looks at his hands, and when they remain there she asks: 'You want me to play? Like this?'

Louka nods. The girl plays, looking provocatively into Louka's eyes.

Who knows what turn the cello lesson would have taken if the telephone had not rung at that moment.

'Louka,' Frank introduces himself.

'This is a friend,' says a male voice in the receiver.

'What friend?'

'Mr Louka, come to the Little City café. This is important,' the voice says urgently.

'Now?'

'It's important. Drop everything and come at once,' the voice repeats.

'Who is this?' Louka wants to know, but the anonymous caller has already hung up. For a while Louka hesitates, the dead receiver in his hand.

Then he picks up the cover of Blanka's cello and says: 'You'll have to come another time, Blanka.'

'That's a pity,' his pupil says.

'You're telling me!' says Louka.

No sooner has he sat down in the café than a man in a nylon blouson with

'Hold it tighter between your legs,' Louka advises Blanka (Sylvia Šuvadová).

a fake sheepskin collar furtively sidles up to him. It is Brož, the grave-digger.

'Come to Schnell's pub,' he says to him, and before Louka can ask why he is gone.

When he finds him at Schnell's he asks: 'Can we sit down here or is there going to be another move?'

Brož looks around him and says: 'It'll be okay here.'

'You're obviously a spy and gravedigging is just your cover,' says Louka, sitting down at a table.

But Brož is in no mood for jokes. He looks him straight in the eye and says: 'Mr Louka, we're in the shit. Nadezhda has emigrated.'

Frank stares at him for a while. The waiter brings them some beer and Louka starts drinking mechanically without taking his eyes off Brož, just as if hypnotized.

'Emigrated to where?' he asks. As if it mattered.

'To West Germany. Went with a group as their interpreter and stayed there. She's got a bloke there. In Frankfurt. I kept that from you. He's a businessman. Married too. She's crazy about him.' Brož spills it all.

'You knew about it!'

'About what?'

'That she has that bloke in Germany.'

'Yes, I knew, but I thought that he'd be coming to see her here. That she went through it all to be closer to him.'

'So why didn't she go and join him straight away?' Louka asks without thinking.

'From Russia to West Germany? Mr Louka, where have you been? They aren't allowed to go there. They can come to us. But not to Germany.'

'I'm surprised our people let her go. She's still a Russian.'

'But she's got Czech citizenship. Thanks to you, that is. And also there is that child she left here. That's why she could go with that tourist group.'

Louka clearly wants to avoid asking how this whole disaster concerns him personally, and so he asks instead: 'And why did she go to join him when he's married?'

'That, Mr Louka, is really no concern of ours,' says Brož wisely. 'What matters now is that the cops will begin to be interested in you. You being her husband, like.'

'I knew I was doing something idiotic. Felt it in my guts,' Louka sighs, crushed.

'I'm very sorry, Mr Louka. Fact. I'd no idea things would take such a turn. But otherwise you're not really involved, you understand? The boy is with the aunt, she's looking after him until the mother claims him back. She's going to apply to the Red Cross, it seems, to get the boy to join her.'

For a little while Louka scratches the damp beer mat with his nail and then he asks: 'And when d'you think I should expect them?'

'Expect whom?'

'Those cops.'

Brož finishes his beer. 'Soon, I'd say.'

The tower room in the Little City is filled with the melancholy minor-key music of the cello. Louka is practising. Outside the window, on the pantiles, the pigeons sit with their heads tucked to one side, as if they are listening. The player stops in the middle of a theme and glances at the door. Maybe he only thought he'd heard a knock. It was probably a beak being rubbed against the metal sill.

Louka plays on. But now somebody really is banging at the door. He puts down his instrument and, bow in hand, walks slowly over to the door.

When he looks through the spyhole he sees two strange men on the landing. The bow slips from his hand and clatters to the floor. Now he has to open up.

'You are František Louka?' says a man with a quilted waistcoat.

'Yes,' admits Louka and swallows hard.

'You are the father of this child?' says the other, who is wearing a white overcoat.

Louka's horrified eyes drop towards the floor. Between the two men stands five-year-old Kolya.

'The father?' says Louka in surprise.

'Listen. Outside, in the ambulance, we have the old lady he lived with. She's had a stroke. And she said you should take him over, see? Here's his things.' And the ambulance man hands Louka the boy's suitcase.

'But I'm only a distant father. I mean, a stepfather,' Louka stammers.

'Look, we don't care, you settle these things within the family. She just

'You get over here this minute and collect him. But this minute,'
says Louka excitedly, meaning the little boy (Andrey Khalimon).

said that while she's in hospital the boy's to stay with you,' the ambulance-man ends the conversation on his way down. Louka, with a strange suitcase in his hand, stares at the backs of the two men as they descend the stairs.

He looks at the child they have left with him.

The boy, as if afraid of his gaze, stares at the closed door. One of his boots is not laced up. He sniffs, and a small bogey disappears up his nostril.

Louka takes a deep breath and says: 'Come along, then.'

The child just stands and stares at the door.

'You can't just stand there. Come inside.' And he opens the door with the notice DON'T RING, KNOCK! even wider.

The child gives another sniff and then shyly enters the strange flat.

Louka doesn't tell Kolya to take off his coat, but leaves the abandoned child standing next to the cello, in his coat and cap, maybe in the vain hope that he won't like it here and that he can send him somewhere else.

He phones, his voice excited: 'Mr Brož, d'you know what's happened? Oh, you do know? In that case you come over here this minute and collect him. But this minute. This isn't part of our deal!'

Brož has a problem telephoning. The weather outside is rough, so he has all the children and all the animals indoors. Mrs Brož tries unsuccessfully to comfort her new twins, who both scream as if they were being slaughtered. To top it all the dog is barking and the bird is screaming 'Bloody job!'

'It would be better not to discuss this on the phone. What's that? Come round tomorrow, Mr Louka, we'll talk about it. Here all hell is let loose. What's that? I don't get you. One night's not going to kill you, is it? Just wash him normally and put him to bed, that's all.'

'Bloody job!' says Louka, slamming down his receiver and beginning to pace up and down the room, followed by the frightened eyes of his small guest. At the window he stops and looks at him. The boy turns his eyes away.

The suitcase is still standing in the middle of the room. Louka moves it to the door and again paces up and down, biting his lips in concentrated reflection. The result of this intensive cerebral activity is meagre: 'Got any slippers?'

Kolya doesn't understand and continues to stand by the cello.

'To put on your feet. Got anything? For indoors?'

The small boy's shoulders shake with sobbing.

'Bloody hell, a fine conversation we two will have.' Louka makes for the suitcase and opens it on his bed. 'That's just what I needed,' he shouts angrily. Just then a pair of slippers appears.

'There you are, you do have some!'

He puts them in front of Kolya and points at them with his finger: 'Slippers! Take your boots off and put the slippers on.'

But the boy doesn't want to stay with this unpleasant, bearded stranger. He just stands there stubbornly and sobs.

There's no other way. Louka will have to touch the child.

He takes off his cap, his scarf, and, when his clumsy fingers have mastered the buttons, he slips his coat off him. On the door not a single hook is free. So he hangs it on the hook where his own overcoat is hanging.

'I expect you can take your boots off yourself, okay? Boots!' Louka's index finger points to the floor.

Maybe he can, but he doesn't want to. The boy is in a state of stubborn refusal of all communication. Louka has to crouch down in front of him. He probably has never taken a child's boot off. One boot already has its laces undone, but the other ties itself into a knot under his fingers.

'Look here. First of all we'll have no blubbing. I'm not exactly over the moon either to have you here. But one night won't hurt you and then you go to the gravedigger's. He's got us into this mess, so he can get us out of it, the idiot!' At last Louka has undone the knot and put the boy into his slippers.

But then what? Louka looks into the suitcase again.

'Great, got some coloured crayons here. And paper.' He puts them on the table. 'Go on, do some pictures. Scribble, scribble, scribble.' He draws some imaginary lines over the paper.

What irritates him most about Kolya is that he is always looking away. Now he's looking out of the window.

'Okay, you just look out of the window. It's all the same to me.'

Louka walks over to the cooker, lights the gas and puts a kettle on. Then he opens the fridge and scratches his head.

He is obviously wondering what to give his unexpected guest. He finds some margarine. He glances at the child. He's still standing exactly where he left him, staring out of the window, like a bird wanting to fly away.

Louka picks up a chair, puts it by the window and without a word places the boy on it as if he were a statue. Kolya stands on the chair just as he had stood on the floor, gazing at the roofs and towers of the city.

A pigeon settles on the window ledge. He picks his plumage with his beak. The boy watches it with sad eyes. It seems that the pigeon in turn is watching him with one eye.

Supper is on the table. Bread and margarine and on it slices of salami. Steam is rising from two mugs of tea.

'Eat,' commands Louka, biting into his piece of bread.

Kolya does not react. He sits facing him, looking somewhere under the table.

'Well at least drink your tea.'

Nothing.

'Tea!' Louka pushes his mug nearer to him. 'It's Russian tea. Surely you lot drink that all the time? Well, drink up, then. Sugar's in it.'

It's all in vain. Louka heaves a sigh and continues eating while he watches the face of the strange child. Then he says: 'Look here. Don't pretend you don't understand. You're bound to understand something. We're both Slavs. Yes, both of us. I don't know Russian and you don't know Czech. But surely you understand "tea". "Tea" is the same in your language as it is in mine. So what about it?'

Louka finishes and carries his plate and mug to the sink to rinse them. When he gets back to the table Kolya is sitting there as before, but his mug is empty.

'There you are,' says Louka, satisfied. 'It's a start, anyway.'

The only light in Louka's tower flat is a little bedside lamp. On the wide bed, constructed for comfortable love-making, Louka listens to Radio Free Europe. There is a lot of fading and at times the station disappears altogether. Far away from him – farther than necessary, right against the wall – lies Kolya. Now and again his shoulders jerk with his sobs. Louka is irritated.

'Don't blub and go to sleep,' he says. 'You'll survive one night.'

He switches off the radio and tries to read an article on Kilimanjaro in a magazine, but his eyes keep turning to the boy's slight back in its flowered pyjamas. He reaches out with his free hand, as if wanting to calm the child by his touch, but then he only pulls the blanket up. When the quiet sobbing doesn't stop he eventually puts his hand on Kolya's shoulder. But the child shakes it off with an angry jerk.

'Leave me alone, then,' he says, offended, and switches the light off.

The faint glow of the city penetrates into the tower flat. The tram can be heard starting from its halt with a hissing discharge between the headgear and the overhead wire. The flash projects Frank's profile on the wall, complete with beard.

With his case over his shoulders and Kolya at his side he steps out on to the pavement. The morning stream of cars is moving down the street. Louka tries to take the boy's hand so they can safely cross the roaring river of metal, but the stubborn child refuses. He keeps close to Louka, out of fear, but he won't give him his hand.

In silence they ride in the Trabant – Louka at the wheel, Kolya in the back. The child's eyes look upwards, watching the receding façades of the tall buildings. As they are waiting at a crossroads a dark-haired young woman, hurrying to work, smiles at the boy and waves to him. Kolya's eyes widen for a second in some vain hope and are instantly extinguished again.

Brož the gravedigger and Louka are walking along a lane in the cemetery. From their gestures you'd say they were quarrelling. The little boy is walking three paces behind them, watching the *art nouveau* tombstones of long-dead Prague burghers.

'She was against it, you know, against my dragging you into that marriage,' the gravedigger says.

'Who was?'

'Maruš, of course, my wife. She said: "Don't be a fool, you'll get him into trouble." '

'And how right she was!' Louka agrees.

'What the hell am I to do with him, Mr Brož?'
Louka desperately asks the gravedigger.

'She was. But now you can't expect her to take on a fifth child. We've got a madhouse already, Mr Louka.'

'And what the hell am I to do with him, Mr Brož?' Louka asks in despair. When he gets no answer he snaps at him: 'What about the one with the gold teeth? Surely she could look after him?'

'Pasha's long gone back to Leningrad,' Brož disappoints him. Then he thinks aloud: 'As I see it, Mr Louka, until they let the aunt out of hospital it'll be best if the boy stays with you. For your sake too. That's why the aunt said to take him to you, see? It's in your own interest. You can now prove that you were in earnest about that marriage since you're actually looking after your wife's child.'

'Who can I prove it to?'

'To them. When they start investigating you. As no doubt they will, Mr Louka. Been there before? For an interrogation, I mean.'

'No.'

'I have. Because of some priest. First cop was sweet as honey. Real polite he was. But then Number Two moved in. Some Novotný. They always use false names. And that one was sharp as a razor. A real bastard. Sooner or later they'll get round to you. They grind slow, like the mills of God,' the gravedigger prophesies, and the big angel on the tomb behind him seems to nod in threatening agreement.

Kolya has hung back, his attention caught by another scene: over a dead white turtle-dove with its head hanging down lifelessly stands a distraught live white turtle-dove, and both are made of marble.

'Come along!' Louka calls out.

The quartet is playing. The little boy is listening to the melancholy music, watching people and things. He sees the ceremonial hall from the organ loft above. He watches the musicians. Most of all he watches Louka who has, as usual, slipped off his shoes and is in his socks.

The child does not miss the hole at the left big toe. The woman singer now joins in and fully absorbs the boy's attention. From her breasts his gaze goes up to her lips which open wider and differently from what is usual, and his gaze meets hers. But her gaze is cold, unresponsive, and soon turns from the boy to her sheet of music.

At the gate of the crematorium Louka and Kolya get into the Trabant. Even before the car moves off Klára crosses in front of its bonnet, deep in conversation with the violinist Pekárek. Louka gives a brief honk. Pekárek turns and waves. But not Klára.

'Mr Louka, you didn't put out those flags,' a female voice laments in the dim light of the landing. 'And you said you would.'

'Didn't get round to it, Mrs Buštíková. Giving concerts for the working people every day . . .' Louka answers shrewdly as he climbs the stairs.

'You're the only one. All the others have. You're a nice little boy. Who d'you belong to?' The woman has noticed Kolya.

'My nephew. Son of my brother,' Louka promptly explains.

'What's your name then?' the woman wants to know.

'He's shy. Comes from the country,' says Louka quickly, pushing the child up the stairs in front of him.

'It's no concern of mine, Mr Louka. But they're going to make a note of it. Needlessly drawing attention to yourself, you are. Needlessly!' Mrs Buštíková's voice dies away as Louka unlocks his door.

But Louka isn't such a hero as he has just made out. As soon as he has put down his cello he draws a chair up to the wardrobe, steps on it and gropes about in the space between two suitcases. Eventually he produces a set of rolled-up little flags.

'I'm a coward.' He blows the dust off and looks for some sticky tape. 'Last year I couldn't be bothered and nothing happened to me. But now that we're in the shit we won't give them a pretext, understand?' the coward justifies himself. On one window pane he sticks the Czechoslovak flag and on the other the red one. At that moment he hears a small voice behind him.

'What's that you said?' He turns in surprise.

The boy stops, but a moment later he points to the left and then to the right flag and says shyly: 'Ours – yours.'

They are the first two words he has spoken to Louka and he has caught him unprepared.

'Quite right. So you see you can speak! Ours – yours.'

And as he takes the boy's coat and cap off he continues with what, in a

61

sense, is a monologue: 'Except we put up yours because we're made to, chum. There was a time when we put it up out of gratitude, before we discovered that you're a lot of shits, you Russians. Understand? No you don't understand. You're expansionists. Wherever you set foot,' Louka pulls off one of the child's boots, 'there you settle for ever. But that's not your case. You're going back to auntie. Soon as she gets better I'll pack your *chemodan* and off you go.'

'*Chemodan*,' the boy responds to the word and points to his suitcase.

'Yup. That's the only word I know because they stole mine at the railway station in Moscow,' Louka says acidly. 'You steal suitcases and other people's territory.'

The two Slavs still don't understand one another, but they have begun to communicate.

Louka puts the food on the table. This time there is a special treat with the tea and bread. 'Look what I've bought for you. A Russian egg.'

'Russian?' Kolya unbelievingly probes it with his fork.

'Sure. Some Czech hens are laying Russian eggs without realizing it.' Louka attacks his plate.

There is a ring at the door.

On the threshold stands a cello in a khaki cover and behind it the long-haired Blanka.

'I've come for my lesson,' she grins.

Louka scratches his head.

'Today?'

'Not convenient?' The girl raises her eyebrows so beautifully that Louka caves in.

'Come on in. But I've got a visitor . . . some . . .'

Blanka catches sight of Kolya at the table and says in surprise: 'Oh hi! Your little boy?'

'No.'

'Grandchild?'

'Friends made me look after him. Musicians from Leningrad. He's Russian.'

'Oh, I see.' And she goes on in Russian: 'Hello, little boy. What's your name?' And she extends her hand.

'Kolya,' says the boy, his mouth full of Russian egg.

As Blanka extracts her instrument from its cover, Louka's gaze encounters the flags on the window. He pulls down the blind so the girl shouldn't see them and turns on the lamp.

'May I?' asks Blanka, gripping her cello between her knees. Louka nods and the beautiful student begins to play scales. Louka corrects the position of her left hand. Blanka's long fingers travel about the fingerboard and Louka's eyes wander from Blanka to Kolya and back again. After a while he gets up and disappears into the bathroom.

To the accompaniment of the scales he turns on the hot and cold taps and starts running a bath.

He returns to the room and beckons to Kolya.

In the bathroom he undresses him and lifts him into the bath. He gives him a face-flannel and soap, and launches a wooden brush like a little boat.

When he sees that the child is happy he leaves.

Kolya obediently soaps himself, fills his flannel with water like a sack and pours it over himself. He attaches a clothes-peg to the brush and the ship has a funnel. Through the door he hears the notes of the cello.

The teacher has put up a stand in front of his pupil and has placed some études on it. He is now standing behind her and from above observes the waving of her hair and her breasts which move with the strokes of the bow. Now he bends over her, takes the bow from her hand and, keeping his pupil between himself and her cello, demonstrates to her how to play the passage.

Kolya is washed, scrubbed clean, and is now inspecting his small fingers which have shrivelled a little from their prolonged immersion. The music in the room has suddenly stopped.

The boy listens to the silence. He shivers a little in the cooling water and looks around for a bath towel. He finds one and rubs himself dry. With the large towel wrapped round him as if it were a cloak he runs out of the bathroom.

The lamp which was on before is no longer on now and the room is in darkness. The little boy steps over the neck of the cello on the floor to get to the window. He pulls the cord and the blind shoots up.

The little boy watches Louka, who for heaven knows what reason has been kneeling beside his wide bed, get up quickly and the naked long-legged girl on the bed hastily pulling the blanket up to her chin.

Blanka looks at the window, where the cord of the blind is still swaying, and sees the two flags. She points at them and laughs: 'So you've put them up after all, Mr Louka!'

Walking together, not hand in hand but next to each other, Louka and Kolya pass the reception desk of the Krč hospital. The porter, using his hands, explains that they must go straight on, then left and then right. They follow his instructions. In his hand Louka carries a bag of oranges. From time to time he reassures himself that they are still on the right way by the signposts with the names of the wards and the symbols for the different departments.

The little boy looks at them too. The letters mean nothing to him but the pictures do. He sees arrows with, next to them, an ear, a nose, an eye, a heart and a child.

In the corridor they put overslippers on over their boots. It takes Louka a while to find the only small pair in which Kolya wouldn't come to grief. They climb up to the next floor and there Louka addresses a nurse. The nurse nods and beckons them to follow her. They enter the ward sister's office.

'Tamara Komarovová?' She looks at Louka severely, then at the oranges he is carrying and then at the small boy. After a moment's hesitation she orders the nurse who has brought them: 'Take the child outside and wait there.'

Kolya joins the nurse willingly enough. He probably thinks she'll take him to the patient.

When the child's been taken outside, the ward sister points with her pencil to an entry in her book, where a discreet little cross has been made.

'She died yesterday. At seven in the morning. You are her – what?'

'Nothing,' says Louka limply. 'An acquaintance.'

'We didn't know whom to inform. We've got her things here. Dressing gown, dentures, spectacles . . .'

Louka no longer hears her voice. He only sees her mouth opening and closing.

Still carrying the oranges he walks out into the corridor. Kolya attaches himself to him, his small head raised questioningly to Louka's grey face.

'Where's *babushka*?' he asks outside, when he realizes that they are making their way back to the entrance hall.

It takes Louka a while to compose an answer.

In the hospital corridor they put on overslippers.

'*Babushka* is asleep. We're not to wake her.'

At the pedestrian crossing the Russian boy sees a traffic sign with an adult leading a child by the hand. This he understands. He puts his hand into Louka's. As this hasn't happened before it rouses Louka from his sleepwalking. He looks down in surprise. The light turns green and hand in hand they cross over.

The shabby office desk next to the crematorium's organ is littered with orange peel. Kolya is finishing his orange and drawing at the same time. He is obviously gifted: his drawings are colourful, but his subjects, monotonously, are memorials with crosses on top and wreaths with ribbons.

'Surely there are those social workers. If I were you I'd apply for the child to be taken into care. Explain he's not your own, that he came with your wife, that his mother's left him and that, with your occupation, you can't look after him properly,' Pekárek the violinist advises.

'Think so?' Louka scratches his chin.

'Or put him in a kindergarten,' suggests Štefl, the second violinist. 'You can't drag the boy from one crematorium to another. Look what he's drawing.' He points to Kolya's sketch, where a coffin is just taking shape.

Klára Koutská is drinking tea and listening with an expression which might be taken for utter indifference, but perhaps also for some satisfaction at what Louka has got himself into.

'Gentlemen, the baking oven won't wait. Let's go,' says the organist from the telephone.

After a few bars of introduction the singer positions herself in front of Louka and sings. Her legs on her high heels guide Louka's eyes up to the hem of her skirt. Louka extends his bow, but misses the skirt and instead nudges Kolya not to lean over the balustrade.

The escalator carries Louka and Kolya up to the concourse of the Prague underground stop called Moscow station. The boy is fascinated by the Kremlin towers on the marble wall. He stops in enchantment to look at this reminder of home. Louka has to come back for him and, taking his hand, leads him out into the street.

The corridor of the children's home is noisy. A group of children is being got ready for a walk and their teacher is unable to control them.

'Auntie, someone's pinched my boot,' a little girl complains, holding one boot in her hand.

'Who's taken Monica's boot?' calls the teacher. 'Tony!'

Kolya watches the hubbub and closes his hand on Louka's.

'You his dad or grandad?' asks a boy chewing gum.

'Grandad,' says Louka softly.

The principal emerges from a door and everything suddenly falls silent. She's got some papers for Louka.

'Fill in these forms and send them to the National Committee, Social Welfare Department, Comrade Zubatá.'

'And when, roughly, can I expect . . .?'

'I have no idea at all,' she says and turns away from him. 'Off you go, children, off you go!'

The Trabant travels along the road we already know. It is lined with ancient trees and leads to Louka's birthplace. Louka is visibly worried, but Kolya absorbs his new world with eager eyes. Bare gnarled branches against a frosty February sky, a dusting of snow blown sideways by the car which leaves a dark track behind on the road surface. A bird of prey perching on a telegraph pole.

In front of the woodpile Louka is chopping pinewood into narrow strips of kindling. Kolya waits while he picks up another log and then tries to stack the kindling.

'I still don't understand it, Frankie,' comes the voice of his mother, who is strewing potato peelings around a bare rose bush. 'You say the boy is Yugoslav. Do you mean his parents have just lent him to you?'

'So he can see something of the Czech countryside,' improvizes Louka.

'But with a name like Kolya, I ask you? That's a Russian name, surely?' The mother goes on digging.

'That I don't know. Kolya is Nikolay. That's a Yugoslav name too.' Louka continues chopping wood.

'That's enough, Frankie,' says his mother, almost as if telling him he should stop lying. But that's not what she means: 'A musician shouldn't do this kind of work. You'll cut off a finger and then what? Did I tell you that uncle Růžička has lost another finger? He's only got six left altogether.'

'No carpenter has all his fingers. A circular saw is the very devil.' Louka is glad that the conversation has moved away from Kolya.

Later indoors, however, over their soup, he brings the talk round to the boy himself.

'Couldn't he stay here for a few days?'

'Who?'

With his eyes Louka indicates whom he means. 'He's pale. Could do with fresh air. And you wouldn't be all alone.'

'What kind of parents are they, those Yugoslavs? Leaving him with strangers!' His mother doesn't understand.

'Musicians. Haven't got time for him. They'd be grateful.'

'Today's young people. Make themselves a child and then don't know what to do with him. If someone wants to dedicate himself to music he shouldn't have children. I must say you've rather sprung this on me, Frankie. And how long would he be staying here?'

'Until I find someone to look after him.'

Up in the attic Louka has to keep his head down so as not to hit a rafter. Kolya, on the other hand, can walk upright, and curiously inspects the strange space where a few shafts of sunlight penetrate the chinks in the roof like long needles. While Frank moves an ancient pair of skis, complete with bamboo poles, to get to a pile of other old junk, such as a retired Blau Punkt radio and two tin gas-mask cases, the boy is enjoying himself with the sunlight: he lets it fall on his shoulder and then retreats until the brilliant spot has travelled down his sleeve to his palm, where it stays like a gold coin. Kolya quickly closes his hand.

Louka has found what he was looking for. It is a flat plywood box with mysterious holes in the top panel. With a sack that is hanging over a beam he wipes off a layer of dust and steps over to the dormer window where there's more light. Curiosity makes Kolya follow him. Louka's hand reaches into the box, and when it emerges again it is holding a figure of Punch. The frozen smile of the old puppet has not lost its magic. The boy's face lights up. Gently he takes the red figure in his hand.

Just as Louka, back in the living room again, is about to insert a forest backdrop into the holes of the portable puppet theatre, the windows start rattling with the deep roar of the engines of an army convoy.

'See them? Always on the move. This way and that,' remarks his mother with a hostile glance towards the window.

Kolya stands on tiptoe to see what's going on outside.

The dark green vehicles with their white stripes and huge wheels roll past, but one comes to a halt. Two soldiers are examining a front tyre.

'Ours,' says Kolya to the old lady.

'Those aren't yours. Those are Russians,' the woman corrects him.

'Come over here. This is the king.' Louka tries to draw the child's attention to another puppet he's just discovered.

But Kolya stays glued to the window.

'Russians!' he says joyously. 'Russian soldiers!'

Old Mrs Louka looks at her son suspiciously.

'What's that he's saying?'

'How should I know? They probably remind him of Yugoslav soldiers. They obviously have similar uniforms,' says Louka, sorting out the tangled strings, so that the puppet of the king accompanies his words with a helpless raising and dropping of its arms.

Before anyone can stop him the boy runs out of the room.

'Kolya! Come back!' Louka shouts after him. But the boy is already in the road and through the window he can be seen in animated conversation with the occupants. The soldiers, delighted to hear their native language, are smiling at him and one of them is lovingly stroking his hair.

Louka avoids his mother's searching gaze and runs out after the boy.

The comradeship, which the old lady is watching through the window

Louka hands the cap back to the soldier and drags the child indoors.

with growing suspicion, has now reached a point where Kolya has a forage cap on his head and is saluting. Louka hands the cap back to the soldier and drags the child indoors.

'You lied to me. He's a Russian,' his mother says drily, still gazing outside.

'I lied to you. He is Russian,' her son answers.

His mother turns in horror, as if she hadn't expected this confession: 'Frankie! You have dealings with them?'

'Mum, not all Russians are the same. His parents . . .' The doorbell cuts short his explanation. He and his mother look through the window. The vehicle is standing there abandoned, without soldiers. There is no doubt who rang the bell. Louka glances at his mother.

'We're not at home,' the wrinkled mouth whispers.

The bell is rung again, this time more urgently.

'Not at home? For heaven's sake, they saw me come in,' says her son and opens the front door.

The two occupants are standing outside, smiling and showing their white teeth and pointing to their blackened hands. 'Good morning,' they say in Russian. 'Could we please wash our hands here?'

'Wash your hands?' Louka makes sure he has understood them. And he would have let the foreign army into the fortress if his mother's uncompromising voice had not come from behind him.

'The water's off.'

'The water is off,' Louka repeats apologetically. 'Mains must have broken somewhere . . .'

'Water is off?' The soldier now understands and, disappointed, looks down at his dirty hands. 'Well, never mind. Thanks all the same,' he says. Then he is gone.

Kolya, who has followed the whole conversation, goes over to the kitchen tap and turns it on.

'It's running!' he says, and his uncomprehending eyes go from Louka to the old lady.

'I'm not having a Russian child in this house,' says the mother. 'That's final.'

Louka takes the child by the hand and says: 'That's it then. Come along, we'll go and see uncle Růžička. You'll like it there.'

As they leave they can hear his mother's receding voice: 'And I'm disappointed in you, Frank. Lying to your own mother! Vic wouldn't do that. You never showed any interest in children, and now suddenly this. A Russian child! It's just as if during the German occupation we'd taken a boy from the *Hitlerjugend* into our home. I wonder what's behind all this . . .'

Uncle Růžička has a stack of planks and squared timbers in his yard. A few new wooden rakes and handles for spades and scythes are leaning against the unrendered brick wall of his workshop.

From behind the sawdust-covered panes in the door comes the whining of a planing machine.

Louka and Kolya enter the sound-filled semi-darkness.

The boy keeps a firm grip on his guide's hand.

Only when Louka's shadow falls across the planing machine does the carpenter with his horn-rimmed spectacles notice that he's got visitors. He straightens up from his work, nods and pushes the timber under the rotating cylinder to its end. Then he reaches down and the noisy machine begins to lose speed.

'How's life, uncle?' Louka asks the old man and from his tone and the way he touches his shoulder it is obvious that he is pleased to see him.

'Well, there's less and less of it, lad,' the uncle says with a wistful smile, and in evidence of it he holds out his hands on which the voracious circular saw has left only six fingers.

Kolya is frightened by the rounded stumps of former thumbs and forefingers and retreats a step.

'Whose boy's that? Not Vic's?' The uncle has noticed the child.

'No. Belongs to friends of mine,' says Louka.

'Well, when you were his age, Frank, you were quite a handful,' the old man reminisces, looking at Kolya's smooth face. 'Instead of going to violin lessons you'd come to me,' the uncle says to the boy, just as if time had turned back and little Frank was visiting him. 'But your mother found out. Your hair was full of sawdust.' The hand with the few fingers ruffles Kolya's hair.

'Uncle, would you still know how to make a top?' Louka asks.

In spite of the fire risk in the space full of wood shavings, varnish and glue uncle Růžička lights a cigarette.

'Nobody wants tops these days.'

'Make one for him,' Louka begs.

'My dear boy.' The carpenter looks at his lathe. 'It's years since I . . .'

*'D'you know what one clairvoyant from the Giant Mountains says?
That the balloon will go up this year,' uncle Růžička (Jiří Sovák)
confides to Louka.*

Then he clears away some rubbish that's lying on top of the lathe and picks up a piece of hardwood.

First through Louka's and then through Kolya's eyes we watch the circular saw cutting a short length from the timber, the cylinder then being fitted into the turning lathe and its obedient cutter shaping it into a cone. Louka watches Kolya and Kolya watches the carpenter as the cutter carves out a spiral groove. The craftsman takes the object out of the lathe and goes over it with sandpaper. Then he blows the dust off it, reaches up to a shelf and with three blows of his hammer fits a tack to its point.

The old crippled hand places the top in the child's palm.

Outside in the yard they try it out. With a string on a piece of wood Louka sends it spinning and keeps it going by whipping it. Kolya likes it. He tries it himself but he doesn't succeed. But he perseveres.

'What's new in Prague?' asks uncle Růžička, watching the boy's efforts.

'In Prague? Same as here,' says Louka.

'D'you know what one clairvoyant from the Giant Mountains says? That the balloon will go up this year.'

'They've been saying that for forty years,' the nephew disappoints his uncle.

'Seems he had a vision of the Communists buying gold bars in large numbers and crossing with them into Russia. But there Gorbachev kicked them in the arse and said: "You leave the gold here and get home in a hurry, all of you." But at home nobody wanted them back, and especially the young people and the hospital nurses rebelled, and so, with all bells ringing, they drove them out and established a reservation for them in Albania, like the Red Indians. That's the vision he had.'

'Why the hospital nurses in particular?' Louka wants to know.

'That, lad, I don't know,' says his uncle.

It is night, and Frank and Kolya are falling asleep on the high old matrimonial beds in Mrs Louka's house. The noise of engines is drawing near.

The headlights of the first vehicle of the column sweep across the ceiling. For a moment the room drops back into darkness, but with every further vehicle the fan of light again opens and closes.

'Ours?' Kolya asks in a half-voice.

'Yes. Yours,' answers Louka.

'Are they going to Moscow?'

'No. They're here forever. Just moving to and fro.'

'They live here?'

'Yes.'

'Like me,' says the boy, closing the nocturnal conversation.

Louka and Kolya are walking through the empty provincial town on a cold February day. In the square Kolya catches sight of the statue of Lenin. He jumps with joy, as if he had met a relation.

'*Dyedushka!*' he exclaims. 'My grandfather!'

'That's not your grandfather. That's Lenin,' grunts Louka.

'Lenin is the grandfather of all little children,' Kolya instructs him.

'I don't know what you're saying, chum, but I think it's nonsense,' Louka says, more to himself.

Then there's something in the display case of the local cinema that fascinates the boy. He stops in amazement and then runs up close to it. We are watching the scene from a distance but from the way Louka is trying to drag the child away and Kolya is resisting for all he's worth, ceaselessly pointing to the stills in the case, it is clear that we are witnessing a major dispute. Approaching closer we can see that Kolya is crying and that the pictures behind the glass invite all children to a series of Soviet cartoon films entitled *Tomcat on the Roof*.

'We're not showing, Mr Louka.' The woman in the ticket office smiles and with undisguised satisfaction displays an untouched book of tickets. 'For lack of interest. The children from the Russian soldiers' married quarters came yesterday. Today not a soul.'

'There's no performance,' says Louka to Kolya and is about to leave.

A new fit of crying stops him.

'How much of an audience d'you need for a performance?' Louka shouts into the little window.

'At least five. But it's a Russian film, Mr Louka, a Russian cartoon film for children. Perhaps you made a mistake. *Angelica* isn't until tomorrow . . .'

'Five tickets in the tenth row.' Louka cuts her short.

The box office lady lets her mouth drop open in surprise.

Then, tearing five tickets from the book, she calls out to a man behind her who is just putting his overcoat on: 'Mr Lánský, don't go off, you're going to project.'

Mr Lánský sticks his bald head out of the box office window to see what idiot is making him stay.

'Hello, Frank,' he says, surprised.

'Hello,' Louka replies, picking up the five tickets.

On the silver screen the tomcat is stalking his prey along the roof ridge to the chimney. Kolya follows the scene, wide-eyed with anxiety. The little bird is sitting on the chimney. Just before the cat leaps the bird flies up and lands on his attacker's tail.

The empty cinema resounds with Kolya's grateful laughter.

Louka watches the boy more than the film. The concentrated childish face shows alternate anxiety and relief, compassion and joy, and it is straightforward and all absolute. The little animals have come from Kolya's distant homeland to make him part of them. The boy is beside himself with happiness. He laughs and claps his hands.

The foyer door opens and the attendant from the balcony slips in. She takes up position next to her colleague from the stalls and the two of them whisper together. One nods while the other shakes her head; they are both looking at Louka.

Louka doesn't care. He has never seen Kolya so happy.

It is early evening. Some cars already have their lights on, others not yet. The Trabant hatchback is returning to Prague. Louka is sitting in it alone.

It looks as if he has after all managed to leave the boy with his old mother. But appearances are deceptive. The child has fallen asleep on the back seat and therefore cannot be seen. But now he is waking up and is squeezing between the front armrests to get closer to the wheel.

'Where is my *babushka*?' he asks in a sleepy voice.

'*Babushka* is sleeping,' the driver replies.

Kolya kneels on the back seat and looks out through the rear window. The street lamps have just come on.

The boy can scarcely drag himself up the stairs. Louka waits for him and then picks him up in his arms.

'Mr Louka, you have a registered letter. I signed for you to save you going to the post office,' Mrs Buštíková informs him from her doorstep.

'Good of you,' says Louka, taking the letter.

'And we were ranked as the second best building for decorations. If old Pech hadn't spoilt it for us, we could have come first. And he was issued flags!'

Before she closes her door she adds: 'That letter's from the police. Parking offence, I guess. You'll have to go there in person now, won't you?'

Louka's knees give under him.

In his flat he puts the letter unopened on the table. He undresses the tired Kolya and gives him a shower in the bath. Awkwardly he dries the smooth little body with a bath towel. He hesitates for a moment before the boy's shrunken little willie but then he dries it, and his little balls.

When he has put the boy to bed he sits down at the table and picks up the envelope. He looks at it from the front and from the back. He weighs it in his hand. Then he finds a spot where the flap isn't quite stuck down and inserts his forefinger. With an almost frightening rending sound he finally opens the letter.

The same rending sound also opens the door into the waiting room in the State Security building and in it appears a smiling man of about thirty-five with a moustache. He extends his hand to Louka and says: 'Pokorný. You'll be Mr Louka, that right?'

'Yes,' says Louka and observes that Mr Pokorný's eyes have come to rest with surprise on little Kolya.

'You've brought . . .'

'He's got no one to look after him,' Louka explains.

'Oh,' the official runs his finger over his moustache, 'but during interrogation he can hardly . . . Comrade!' Pokorný calls to the woman at the door. 'We'll leave the child with you.'

'Not possible. He's not used to strangers. He'd howl the place down,' Louka warns.

As if he has understood, Kolya catches hold of Louka's hand.

'Well, yes, dammit.' Pokorný gets flustered. 'You've never been here before?'

'No.'

'You can't do that to us, with the child I mean . . . Okay, come up, both of you. What am I to do with you?'

From his bunch of keys Pokorný selects the key to the lift, opens the door and the three of them step into the small cabin.

'Well, this has never happened before, I can tell you.' Pokorný shakes his head, looking at Kolya.

'You have no children?' Louka asks boldly.

'Yes, I have, but I don't take them to work with me. Maybe Jitka could in the meantime . . .' it occurs to Pokorný as the lift stops.

At the end of the corridor, where Pokorný greets two of his colleagues with the Communist salute and one of them more informally, is a grille with a door in it. Pokorný takes another key from his bunch and unlocks it. With a special key he finally opens the door to his office.

It is sparsely equipped with light-oak veneer furniture. At a small typing desk sits a girl of about twenty. She has just finished an eclair and fishes some flimsy paper out of a drawer to wipe her sticky fingers.

'Good morning,' Louka greets her.

The typist does not react because she has just pitched the crumpled paper into the waste basket.

'Jitka, you'll have to look after this boy. Why not take him next door to Kopecký's office? He's not there,' Pokorný tells her.

Jitka does not seem enthusiastic about this unaccustomed task.

She opens the door to the corridor and says to Kolya: 'Come along then!'

Kolya holds on to Louka's hand and looks up in fear at his stepfather.

'You go along with auntie. She'll play with you.' Pokorný nudges him.

But as soon as he touches him the boy bursts out howling. The note gets stronger and higher like a siren.

'He won't go,' says Louka. 'He's afraid of strangers.'

'How old is he then?' Pokorný is astonished.

'Five,' says Louka. 'But he doesn't understand Czech anyway. He's Russian. So that should make it okay for him to be here, shouldn't it? If you had a piece of paper and a pencil he'd be quite happy drawing.'

Pokorný sighs helplessly and with a gesture orders Jitka to provide the articles asked for. Kolya is given paper and a pencil and made to sit at a small table by the door.

'You wouldn't have any coloured crayons? He likes pastels,' Louka says daringly in a half-voice, but the typist does not react at all. She is either deaf or stupid.

Pokorný sits down behind his desk and motions Louka to sit down facing him. He puts his key-bunch down by his right hand and lights a cigarette. He glances into a slim folder and shakes his head in amusement. Then he looks up and smiles at Louka quite pleasantly.

'So you got married, Mr Louka!'

'Yes,' Louka admits.

'How come, how come? Never before felt inclined to do so, a dyed-in-the-wool bachelor, and suddenly at fifty-five . . .'

Louka shrugs: 'Just came over me. A man does stupid things. In his dotage.'

'Well, she's pretty, I grant you that,' says Pokorný, studying Nadezhda's photo. 'And young . . . A fellow can fall in love before he knows what's hit him.'

'That's just it,' Louka agrees. The pleasant tone of the interrogation confuses him a little.

'How did you actually meet, Mr Louka?'

'In a restaurant.' Louka was prepared for this question.

'What restaurant was that?'

'The Little City café. She was sitting at a small table, there wasn't anywhere else free, so I joined her. And one word led to another . . .'

'You speak Russian well?'

'That's just it. I don't. Only what one remembers from school.'

Louka notices that the interrogator's desk has brown scorch marks in several places. And now another cigarette has dropped from the rim of the ashtray, making a new blister.

'Cigarette,' he says to the interrogator.

'You'd like one? Help yourself.' Pokorný offers him a full packet.

'No. I meant it's dropped on your desk.'

'Oh that? Happens all the time.' The official stubs it out and lights another.

Kolya comes over to Louka to show him what he has drawn.

It is, needless to say, a grave with a cross. But next to it is a more positive drawing of a cello.

'Nice,' Louka commends him.

In the office next door sits a man with thinning hair and rimless glasses. He is cutting his nails while listening to the conversation on his loudspeaker.

'Let's see,' he hears Pokorný's voice. 'The boy draws very well. This violin here . . .'

'It's a cello. It's got a spike here,' Louka's voice corrects.

'Ah yes. Violins don't have that. Or the player would stab himself,' Pokorný giggles in the speaker.

Novotný finds the level of the interrogation next door too much for him.

'I have a boy of five too, but he wouldn't draw as well as this,' Pokorný is heard saying.

'What's his name?' asks Louka.

'Radek. After my wife.'

'Your wife is called Radek?' asks Louka in amazement.

'My wife is called Radka.'

This is definitely too much for Novotný. He is the second player, whose job it is to wait till the citizen is lulled into a sense of security by the first player's affability.

Then he will burst into the arena and crush his unprepared opponent with a few hard strokes. Captain Novotný switches off his loudspeaker in disgust, clears his throat to make sure his voice is resonant at his entry, picks up his bunch of keys from his desk and leaves his office.

'Morning. What gives?' he says in the doorway of Pokorný's office.

'This is Captain Novotný, Mr Louka,' Pokorný introduces him.

Louka gets up, maybe to shake hands with Novotný, but Novotný flings his keys on Pokorný's desk, places himself by the window so that the person under interrogation will have to look into the light, and hits out straight away: 'Listen, my dear good man, you seem to have a bad influence on your family, what? First your brother emigrates, and now your wife has emigrated . . . What?'

Louka shrugs.

'You didn't live together long after that wedding, in that tower of yours? Leastways no one has seen her there.'

'We did live together for a few days, yes, rather, but we didn't really understand one another. She speaks Russian, I speak Czech . . .' Louka tries his fairytales on him.

'I suppose you didn't notice before your wedding that she didn't understand Czech.'

'Yes, I noticed all right, but there were also other things we didn't agree on. For instance, she was forever opening the window, being used to the cold from Siberia . . . So we said to each other that we'd live apart,' Louka rambles on.

'Okay. Jokes are over now and the serious business begins,' Novotný says with unexpected sharpness, picking up his keys from the desk.

'How much did you get for that tomfoolery?'

Louka is alarmed. He looks instinctively at Captain Pokorný, who's treated him so amicably, as if expecting help from him against this ruffian. But the nice captain shows no inclination to help.

'I asked you a question.'

Kolya senses that the new person is hostile to Louka. He leaves his drawing and sits himself on Louka's lap to protect him.

'Comrade, can't you take the child . . .?' Novotný turns to the typist.

'No use, Vlasta. We've tried it,' Pokorný intervenes.

'Where did you get the money for that Trabant?' the nasty captain resumes. He rattles his keys at regular intervals as if measuring time with them.

'Some of it I'd saved and some I borrowed,' Louka answers without hesitation. That was a question he was prepared for.

'From whom?'

'My colleague Pařízka and Mr Brož.'

Kolya senses that the new person is hostile to Louka.
He leaves his drawing and sits himself on Louka's lap.

'Did Bilyukova confide in you that she intended to emigrate?' Kolya hears his mother's name and looks up questioningly at Louka.

'No. It came as a surprise.'

'And that she left her child to you also came as a surprise?'

'That too.'

'What do you intend to do with him?' Novotný points to Kolya with his chin.

'I don't know. Probably keep him with me. After all, he came with my marriage.'

'Listen, my dear good man. That marriage was a sham if ever there was one,' says Novotný. 'And those stories of the old goat falling in love you can tell to the marines. And before we lock you up don't think you'll be playing with the Philharmonic. Fiddle at funerals at the most. We'll see to that.'

Pokorný, who is evidently better informed, writes something on a piece of paper and gives it to Novotný. What it says is

HE ONLY PLAYS IN CREMATORIUMS

'The comrade captain is rightly angry, Mr Louka,' the nice Captain Pokorný bridges the pause. 'You might perhaps come out of this with your skin intact if you told us honestly, man to man, how it all was, who arranged the wedding, what bribe you got to go through with it, simply man to man.'

'Well, this is certainly not our last meeting. You go home and think it over, and maybe before we invite you again you'll come on your own initiative, that option exists,' says Novotný, glancing at his watch. He probably has something more important to concern him.

'Let's write it all up then, comrade.' Novotný turns to the typist who is just yawning.

'Louka František, having been summoned, states in evidence that . . .'

The typewriter starts rattling and we can leave the office where the person summoned has had such an unpleasant time.

Louka steps out of the hateful building and walks with Kolya along Bartolomějská Street.

'Well, that's over then,' he breathes.

'Well, that's over then,' unexpectedly comes a childish voice from Louka's right side. With just a slight Russian accent.

Louka pays no attention to Kolya's first Czech sentence, and so the little boy adds something from Captain Novotný's repertoire: 'My dear good man,' he says calmly, looking up at his stepfather.

Only now does Louka realize what has happened. And he pulls up sharply.

'Well done! Two or three more interrogations and you'll be speaking Czech.'

He takes his little Russian by the hand and smiling with sudden relief he makes for Petřín Hill.

In the shoe shop Louka buys Kolya a pair of light shoes for the spring. He checks whether they fit him at the toes. The boy walks shyly up and down with them. He looks at Louka and nods. Louka looks at the girl assistant and nods. The assistant nods also.

Kolya keeps his new shoes on. Louka has his boots put into the shoebox and tied up with string.

The underground carriage is packed. Louka and Kolya have to stand.

Facing Kolya sits an old lady. A puppy's head is peeping out of a shopping bag on her lap. The young dog and the boy study each other.

After a while someone slaps Louka's shoulder. It is an attractive woman of about thirty with hair the colour of honey.

Under her arm she carries a violin case. Louka's face lights up with pleasure at this unexpected meeting. They make a space for themselves among the crowd and start chatting. From their looks and from the way that Louka permits himself to take her flowing hair into his hand it is clear that they know each other well.

The old lady has meanwhile allowed Kolya to stroke the puppy. His hand first cautiously touches its little snout and then caresses it between the ears.

Louka's dormant weakness for women has evidently awoken. He is probably saying something amusing to her, because the violinist's mouth is wide open in laughter, bending her head down happily as if taking a shower under the waterfall of his words.

The loudspeaker announces Můstek station and Louka, deep in conversation, gets out together with the honey-haired girl.

Not until he's taken a few steps and the platform speakers announce: 'Mind the doors. The doors are closing,' does Louka glance at the box in his hand and stop as if rooted to the spot.

'The boy,' he gasps.

'What's that?' The violinist doesn't understand.

'Forgive me,' Louka manages to utter, and while the stream of passengers is carrying the girl towards the exit, he desperately fights his way against the current to the train with Kolya.

But the doors, as the loudspeaker announcement warned, have just closed and the train is accelerating into the dark tunnel. Louka, the shoebox in his hand, stares after it. He is utterly helpless.

Kolya meanwhile is playing with the puppy. Now he is looking to his left, maybe to show off to Louka his new friendship with the little dog. Next to him stands a gentleman reading a newspaper. Kolya can't see his face and, suddenly becoming unsure, steps up close to him. From beneath he sees a strange face with glasses and frighteningly hairy nostrils. The boy looks about himself in alarm. With uncertain steps he makes his way through the moving carriage. He pushes between the trouser legs of passengers and desperately seeks the bearded face of his guardian.

Louka has decided to confide in the duty inspector of Můstek station. Her lips slowly articulate into a microphone: 'A five-year-old boy has got lost on Line B. He does not speak Czech. He answers to the name of Kolya. Please take him to the duty inspector at any station.'

Louka pushes forward to the microphone and says in a mixture of Czech and Russian: 'Kolya, don't be afraid and don't run away. Simply stay in the Metro and we'll find you. *Zdravstvuy.* End of our transmission in the Russian language.'

The duty inspector grins and takes over the microphone: 'I repeat our announcement . . .'

At the end of the line the carriage empties. Kolya is the last to get out. By now he is crying silently.

The station relays the announcement about him, but against the noise of a train arriving from the opposite direction it can't be made out.

Kolya, guided perhaps by an instinct to return to where he has come from, gets on.

When the inspector in her glass booth shrugs her shoulders to say that the search has brought no results, Louka makes for the escalator and rides down, overtaking those in less of a hurry.

At the last moment he jumps into a train whose doors are just closing.

The train hurtles through its tunnels. It has left the tiled walls intended for the public and dimly lights up a tangle of service cables and tubes. Louka is tortured by the slowness of the train which, in fact, is travelling very fast. He looks at his watch and presses the children's shoebox to his chest, as though someone might wish to steal it.

'Moscow station,' says the loudspeaker in the carriage eventually. Louka roughly pushes through the alighting passengers to make sure he is the first out. The string on his box breaks and Kolya's old lace-up boots fall to the ground. Louka picks them up from the platform, between the feet of indifferent travellers. One is kicked away and he finds it by a pillar, where a uniformed woman employee of the Metro is standing.

'You haven't by any chance seen a boy here?'

'How old?'

'To fit into these boots.' He pushes Kolya's boots under her nose.

'The one who doesn't speak Czech?'

'That's the one,' Louka says hopefully.

'There was an announcement about him. But I haven't seen him.'

In the street-level entrance hall of Moscow station Louka, exhausted and with his box under his arm, stops and obstructs the traffic. He doesn't care and patiently looks all round him. Nothing.

He asks the newsvendor; he asks the man selling lottery tickets; he asks a traffic policeman. With his left hand he shows them the child's boots and with his right he indicates his height. In vain.

His heart is pounding so loud that everybody must hear it. Louka leaves the vestibule and stands on the pavement. Some woman is dragging a little boy to the tram stop. Louka catches him by the shoulder and spins him round. He is a strange child with freckles.

Resigned, he returns to the entrance of the Metro. For a while he stands in the middle of the stream of people and then he decides to make one last effort. He takes a deep breath and yells so loud that those near him jump with fright: 'K-o-l-y-a!!!'

His voice reverberates through the vestibule and from under the plastic fresco of the Kremlin towers something that looks like a forgotten piece of luggage gets up and, in squeaky new shoes, races towards him.

Louka presses the child to him and holds him in his embrace longer than one might expect from a stranger.

'Phew, you gave me a fright!' he says, and his eyes are moist – which at his age is excusable.

♪ ♫ ♪♪ ♫ ♪♪

Louka's little brush is gilding the lettering on a tombstone. It is a sunny day in March.

'That wasn't a telephone call, Mr Louka, that was one long wail over the wire,' the gravedigger reports.

'So what did she say?' Louka wants to know.

'*Kolyenka*, my little one, darling . . . When I told her the aunt had died and the boy was with you she nearly fainted. Said she'd go straight to the station and take the next train, real hysteria. Of course, I dissuaded her. I said: "Don't be daft, they'll nick you as soon as you cross the frontier and send you straight to the camp in the Urals." '

'And what about the Red Cross?'

'She applied the moment she got to Germany. It can't take long now, Mr

Louka. The child must go to his mother. They have international agreements on this. And she sends you her best regards.'

'Isn't that nice of her,' grins Louka.

A little way off Kolya is playing with Ládík. They are throwing a small withered wreath across the truck like a frisbee.

'I told them that you lent me money,' Louka reminds him.

'I told them the same.'

'You've already been there?'

'No. They came to me. Captain Nice and Captain Nasty. It's the boy you're looking after, Mr Louka, that's bothering them. This is where we cooked their goose. And you come out of it clean, simply as a fool who allowed himself to be conned.'

'You couldn't have put it better,' Louka agrees.

'The child's got to join his mother,' Brož repeats, watching Kolya's vain attempts to catch the wreath in flight. 'Can't take much longer now, Mr Louka.'

Louka is getting supper. The same as always – tea, bread and margarine and salami. This time the extra will be hard-boiled eggs. As he is peeling the shells off he hears Kolya's voice from the bathroom. With his foot he slightly opens the gap in the door and looks in.

The naked boy is sitting in the bath, with the hand shower held to his ear like a telephone.

'*Babushka*? This is me, Kolya. *Zdravstvuy*! I want to come to you, *babushka*. D'you hear? We went to see you but you were asleep. Come and see us!'

Louka enters the bathroom. Tears are running down Kolya's cheeks.

'Come along.' Louka opens the bath towel and, wrapping it round the boy, lifts him out to the edge of the bath. First he wipes his tears.

Kolya is in bed and Louka is on the telephone.

'Susie? I suddenly felt so melancholy and who d'you think . . . ? Can you talk? Where is he? In Bath? Aren't you lucky. Oh, in the bath. But he soaks himself for a long time, what? Look, Susie, I'm looking after a Russian child. Yes, Russian. Of a violinist in Leningrad. And he won't go to sleep. Listen, you teach Russian, don't you? Couldn't you read him a story? Just so. Over the telephone. Five years. Doesn't matter what. Find something, I'll wait.'

Louka turns to Kolya who, from sheer boredom, watches the shadow of his hand on the white wall.

'There's a teacher there.' He points to the telephone. 'She'll tell you a story.'

'What?' Kolya doesn't understand.

'Once upon a time.'

By now Susie has returned to the telephone.

'The eagle and the little lamb? Sounds terrific.' Louka is delighted. 'I'm handing him over to you.'

As soon as the boy hears his native language he comes to life. Politely he answers the strange voice: 'Yes. Kolya Bilyukov. No, I'm not afraid of eagles.'

Then he listens with a happy smile.

'High up in the Caucasus mountains there lived an eagle. He liked flying high, very high . . .' A heavily accented tale as old as the hills flows into the child's parched soul.

Let's just see what's happening at the other end of the line.

The teacher, a well-preserved woman in her forties in a pretty housecoat, is totally absorbed in the story of the eagle and the little lamb.

'One day he flew so high that he came to a star. On that star there was a little house . . .'

The dramatic recital brings the husband from the bathroom. He moves furtively to discover at whom his little dove is cooing this time. He stops drying his hairy body and listens: 'And in it lived an old ewe with her little lamb. "I'm here on a visit," said the eagle.'

The husband shakes his head uncomprehendingly and retreats to the bathroom.

'Lovely,' breathes Kolya, by now half asleep, and the receiver slips from his hand.

'Thank you,' Louka says softly into the receiver and is about to hang up, but Susie has something else on her mind.

'You left them here, at my place?' Louka asks under his breath. 'Black ones with lace? And you actually went home without them? Susie, I would have noticed a pair of panties. I'd love to see you, Susie, but I can't. I'll be in touch. So long.'

Then he pulls the blanket over the boy. For a while he stands looking at his calm sleeping features.

For once the quartet up in the organ loft of the Strašnice Crematorium is playing some non-funeral music. The organist is not involved, so he is having a snack while, at the same time, doing a crossword. Kolya, his elbows on the balustrade, watches the flower-covered coffin receding offstage and the curtain slowly closing.

Next to him Klára Koutská is munching an apple. She has one left and offers it to him. Kolya shakes his head.

From the window of Louka's flat it is obvious that spring has taken possession of Prague. In the Ledebur garden the trees are in blossom, the verdigris on the towers is a brilliant green in the young sun. The boy is standing on a chair by the window, feeding the pigeons. They are used to him by now and fearlessly come quite close.

Louka, maybe to keep in form for better times, practises some difficult composition, one that is certainly boring for Kolya. As he turns a page he says: 'Don't keep feeding those pigeons. We'll have too many of them. And do shut the window, my feet are cold.'

And he continues to conjure up heartrending tones from his strings.

Kolya obeys and looks for something that would amuse him. Then he withdraws to the corner where he has his crayons and where, on a low table, stands the puppet theatre from Louka's own childhood. He takes a wooden clothes peg and colours it green, yellow and red.

The shoebox is also lying there and the boy now begins to draw on it.

Let's leave him without supervision for the moment and watch the cellist, his feet in socks which again are holey, his hands and his concentrated features, in order to be the more surprised by Kolya's final oeuvre.

Now it is finished. Fixed with the multicoloured clothes peg to the right proscenium arch of the puppet theatre is a black-framed sheet of paper with the drawing of a red figure on it. The shoebox, painted with bouquets, wreaths and ribbons, is slowly receding into the backdrop of the inferno and the little curtain slowly closes behind it. In front of the little theatre, with their lifeless heads hanging, sit the mourners – the king, the princess, Škrhola, Šmidra, Dumb Honza and the Devil. All this is accompanied by Louka's sad violoncello.

When the curtain parts again and the ceremony is repeated Louka looks at it. Cursorily at first, but presently his eyes swing back to it.

The paper coffin is just jerking along towards the infernal fire and the little curtain begins to move.

Louka stops playing. He gazes in surprise at this morbid childish performance, absently puts his cello into the corner and steps closer.

'What on earth is all this?'

'*Rabota tvaja* – your profession,' Kolya explains guilelessly.

With his bow Louka raises the lid of the coffin to see who the deceased is. It is Punch. And what's that black veil he's covered with? Aghast, Louka with the tip of his bow lifts up a pair of ladies' knickers, black ones with lace.

Holding the deceased Punch in one hand and the panties in the other, the cellist stares at the child, not knowing what to do. Then he strikes the decorated box with his bow and with sudden resolve says: 'Now that's enough!'

After this, Louka embarks with some gusto on showing the child a different side of life.

All those stairs! Kolya is climbing the viewing tower on Petřín Hill and urges his breathless stepfather to hurry up.

What a height! And what a wind! From the viewing tower Louka shows the boy the city of Prague.

'This is our capital. D'you know how many towers it has? A hundred!'

With one swift movement the barber puts a white sheet around Kolya and cuts his hair. Louka indicates how he wants the ears done.

A train roars over the railway bridge, hooting. Our two friends stand close to each other by the railing, covering their ears with their hands.

The photographer places Kolya in an armchair, puts a red bus in his hand and turns his head to one side. When he has coaxed an unnatural smile out of him he clicks the shutter and the picture is ready.

And now something totally new: Kolya in the kindergarten. Beyond the fence he is playing in the sandpit with some little girls. Louka greets the nursery teacher. She puts her hand to her mouth and Kolya turns his head. He sees Louka, throws down his spade and runs over to him.

All fun must come to an end. Kolya is sick. He's in bed and a thermometer sticks out of his mouth. When Louka pulls it out and examines it under the lamp the red column stands at forty.

A nervous finger runs down a page in the telephone directory and then dials a number.

A medical bag is resting on the sheet and the woman doctor now opens it. Kolya's mouth likewise opens and a little mirror throws light into it. A stethoscope moves over the small boy's back. Kolya takes a deep breath.

'Looks like a sore throat,' the paediatrician says. 'Mother's not at home?'

'The mother is not in town . . . She's temporarily abroad,' Louka says.

'I see. Well, we'll give him an antibiotic.' She writes something on a carton of tablets. 'Every four hours. Better set your alarm. And with it always a quarter of an aspirin. You've got some aspirin?'

'Yes. We've got that.'

'There's always a risk of meningitis. If his temperature doesn't come down give him cold packs. Know how to do this?'

'Packs? Oh yes,' says Louka unconvincingly.

The doctor eyes him curiously.

'Your wife will be away long?'

'Probably quite some time.'

'So you'll need a childcare slip for your employer, won't you?'

'I suppose so.' Louka has no experience of this.

'Very well, I'll be looking in tomorrow in any case,' says the lady doctor while writing out the chit.

The boy's breathing becomes fast and he hallucinates.

He sees before him an angel with outspread wings, one he has seen in the Vinohrady cemetery. From below he looks at his stone face and he sees the large nostrils and face of the strange gentleman with the newspaper.

He is blindly wandering about the carriage between trouser legs and shopping bags. The train emerges from the Metro tunnel and rushes straight at him.

Louka sits Kolya up and gives him his medication. The child washes it down thirstily and falls asleep again.

Kolya is alone on an empty station platform.

On the big flagstones his top is spinning. There is the whine of a circular saw. Uncle Růžička's fingerless hand reaches out for the top and flings it away.

It is caught by Pasha who laughs through her gold teeth. Behind her aunt Tamara appears. She smiles and beckons him to her.

Louka puts his hand on the boy's forehead.

'Shhhh,' he calms his incomprehensible raving.

Then he looks at the telephone. And then at his watch. And then at the thermometer. The red column has climbed to forty-one.

Louka picks up the telephone.

Organ music sweeps through Kolya's dreams. The curtain rises and his mother's face appears. A ring is slipped on Louka's finger and gets stuck at his knuckle. The bearded man kisses his mother.

The lion in the coat-of-arms opens his mouth and roars because the tomcat from the cartoon film approaches him. The Russian and the Czech animal attack one another.

'His temperature hasn't gone down, so I got alarmed.' Louka's voice is heard against the receding organ.

'He's had aspirin?' a woman's alto asks in the receiver.

'Yes. A quarter. But I don't know how to do those cold packs. She talked about some packs . . .'

Louka is holding the child in his arms and Klára Koutská is spreading a wet sheet on the bed. When Louka puts the child on it he lets out a yell at the sudden chill.

'Be a brave little boy now. This'll make you better,' the woman reassures him, wrapping the shivering little body in a big bath towel.

Having covered the patient up to his chin she sits down beside him.

'So far so good,' says Louka and turns to Klára: 'Thank you. And I'm sorry to have called you out like this in the middle of the night.'

'Don't give it another thought. That's quite all right.'

'No, it really is . . . many thanks. And good night . . .' Louka is about to shake hands with her.

'You don't have to send me away. I'll stay here till the morning,' Klára announces calmly.

'And what will you say at home?'

'That one of my former lovers has acquired a child through marriage and can't cope with him.' Klára wipes a drop of perspiration from Kolya's forehead.

The town is plunged into darkness. The clock on the tower strikes one. The

'You don't have to send me away. I'll stay here till the morning,'
Klára announces calmly.

car park attendant in his little box pours himself some tea from his thermos. A publican turns a drunken guest out into the street and locks up.

'A magpie or a jackdaw,' says Klára, sitting in the darkened room with a blanket over her knees, facing Louka. She inspects the jewel from the guttering. 'They steal shiny things.' After these words she hiccups.

'That's an idea. Nobody thought of that,' Louka says, surprised.

'But it's beautiful, even if it's got no value.' The singer lets the trinket glitter under the little lamp and puts it back on the table.

When she has hiccuped again she remembers something: 'When I said that we can't have children, my husband and me, this doesn't mean that I can't have children. You probably misunderstood at the time.'

'When's he due for his next tablet?' Louka changes the subject.

'Five in the morning. The alarm's set.'

'Aren't you tired? You can sleep if you like.' He points to the bed.

'I don't want to sleep. I've always wanted to spend a whole night with you, so at least my wish is being fulfilled.'

Louka doesn't know what to say, so Klára continues: 'But you're not as selfish as I thought. Wouldn't have thought you'd worry so much about a strange child.'

'You know what? I wouldn't have thought so myself,' Louka admits.

'One more thing. Please explain to me how you weren't afraid of that marriage fraud? You, a political persecutee who's not allowed out to the West?' Klára wants to know.

'I'm not a political persecutee. I'm persecuted because of my own stupidity. They let me go to Austria with the Philharmonic. Once. Our political minder, Bláha, said to me: "Comrade, your brother has emigrated, but we've decided to trust you." When we got back I had to fill in a questionnaire. It asked had I met any emigrés there? I said, yes. And then it said: Give details of what you talked about. And I wrote: "Shit, more or less, Comrade Bláha." '

'That's all?'

'Probably he was offended and that was that.'

'Heavens, and I thought God knows what you'd been up to.'

Klára gets up and looks out of the window into the dark.

'Pitiful, isn't it?' says Louka behind her.

After a moment the woman turns unexpectedly and kisses him. 'You filled it in perfectly.' She smiles at him.

Louka lays the cheap trinket from the guttering on her palm.

'I'd like you to have it,' he says.

Kolya takes his tablet and washes it down.

The worst is over. He still has a poultice round his neck, but he is sitting up in bed, drawing. When Louka picks up the alarm clock to set it for the next penicillin the boy shows him his picture.

'Very nice. At last you've given up those coffins,' Louka commends him and wants to move away.

But the child catches hold of his pullover and again shows him his drawings. There is a black bird, probably an eagle, and next to it a lamb, and next to that a telephone.

'Yes, I can see. Animals . . . very nice.' Louka praises it once more.

With a crayon Kolya points to his picture of the telephone and in a croaky voice explains: 'The story from the telephone.'

'Yes, now I get it.' Louka understands. 'You'd like a story over the telephone. Let's dial the auntie teacher then . . .' And he reaches for the receiver.

When he gets through an unpleasant, strident male voice answers: 'Samohýl. Who's that speaking?'

Louka hangs up.

'That was the uncle. He's no good at stories,' says Louka, stretching out by Kolya's side. After a while he says: 'Why not try it ourselves? Once upon a time there was a grandad and a granny. Understand?'

'*Dyedushka* and *babushka*.' The boy nods.

'Well done. They had a grandson whose name was Budulínek.'

'Budulínek,' Kolya repeats with a smile.

' "Listen, Budulínek," his granny says to him one day. "We're going into town and you'll be here on your own. You're not to open to anyone . . ." '

'Not open to anyone . . .'

Louka holds on to its sidewall, which is forbidden.

The Trabant speeds along a road between golden corn fields.

The oil can in Louka's hand releases golden drips into the chain of the dusty old bicycle that has been lying in the attic for years. Kolya uses a rag to revive the fading rubies of the rear reflectors. Louka's fingers are testing the hardness of the tyres.

And already they're riding out of the gate. Old Mrs Louka steps out of their way and looks after them with the uncomprehending eyes of one betrayed. Louka pedals cheerfully while Kolya sits on the frame in front of him.

The sunlit track, whose ditches are alive with crickets, runs slightly downhill. The bike is gaining speed, the riders are shouting something to each other but the wind carries their words away. Kolya is filled with the euphoria of speed, and Louka would be happy too if he weren't so desperately holding on to the handlebars for fear that they'll come a cropper at the bottom.

As they walk uphill Louka leans the bike against a post and the two of them together pee into the beautiful valley.

And they're off again. On the way up a tractor with a trailer overtakes them. With his right hand Louka reaches out for its sidewall, which is forbidden, and lets himself be pulled. The driver turns his head and smiles approval.

They take a rest on the grass verge. They eat cherry cake. Kolya observes a bumble bee eagerly dipping into a clover blossom. Louka observes two girls in fashionable cut-off shorts with backpacks who have just walked past them. Then he flicks a cherry stone at Kolya.

'And how do you see the future with that child, Frankie?' his mother asks in the evening as they sit facing each other at the table. 'Surely you can't go on like this. So how do you see it? What will you do with him?'

'Do with him?' Louka muses. 'Tomorrow we'll set out for the Vydra. Remember that river in the Šumava mountains where we holidayed in forty-seven? He'll enjoy that, I think.'

The rustle of the mountain stream rises from the canyon. From the top of a tall tree, where a squirrel is just demolishing a pine cone, we can see the Vydra river. The water flows over and around huge boulders, breaks into spray and creates whirlpools.

On a large flat rock, as on a hotplate, lie two bodies on their stomachs. A long one and a short one. Let's get closer to them.

'There used to be otters in this river. That's why it's called Vydra, or otter river.'

'Otters,' Kolya repeats. '*Shto takoye* – what's that?'

'You and your eternal *shto takoye*. An animal, about this size.' Louka indicates with his hands. 'And bearded, like me. And these otters ate the trout.'

'*Shto takoye?*'

'Trout are fish.'

'Fish.' Kolya understands. Luckily 'fish' is the same in Czech and Russian.

'That's right. And because the water is now acid from all that acid rain – you can't understand that because I don't understand it myself – all the fish perished. Died. Fish kaput. And as a result the otters also perished.'

'Otters also kaput?' Kolya asks sadly.

'Very good. So the river is still called Vydra, or otter river, but there are no otters here now. That's the kind of river we have.' And Louka puts his hand into the transparent dead water.

'Vydra,' Kolya repeats for himself.

In the campground the Trabant stands next to a small tent. Through the summer evening comes music from transistor sets and a distant live guitar.

Louka and Kolya sit facing each other at a small fire, grilling small sausages. Kolya's drops into the fire.

'Well, that's that,' he says in Czech.

Together they walk through the darkening campground between cars and trailer caravans, between luxurious tents with foretents and TV sets, they duck under guy ropes with wet swimming trunks on them, they dodge the blue flames of gas burners with bubbling tinned stew on them. A group of Germans are singing: '*Alles Gute für dich, Helmut . . .*'

'Some East German celebrating his birthday,' remarks Louka.

'*Shto takoye?*'

'The day on which you were born.'

'*Den' razhdeniya?*' Kolya has understood. After a few steps he stops. 'When will I have my *den' razhdeniya*?'

'When were you born?'

The Russian boy shrugs.

'You've got a problem then,' Louka laughs. 'You want to celebrate your birthday but you don't know when you were born.'

The two brush their teeth over the tin trough in the washroom.

Louka pulls down the entrance zip and it's almost dark in the tent.

He also pulls up the zip on Kolya's sleeping bag.

'Good night,' he says.

'Good night, Dad,' answers Kolya.

For a while they lie quietly, then the boy raises himself and kisses Louka's jaw where he has no beard.

This has obviously not happened before. On his back Louka looks at the tent canvas through which comes the glow of their neighbours' fire.

'We shall overcome, we shall overcome,' promises the spiritual.

But it is overlaid by the speaker of some radio station: 'He who sows the wind shall reap the whirlwind, the workers of the Tlak factory declare in their resolution. We will not let anyone undermine our Republic . . .'

A glance from the window of Louka's tower flat reveals that summer has said farewell to Prague and left the trees to the rough mercies of autumn.

Kolya blows out five candles on a cake.

'Above all, be well and cheerful,' is Louka's birthday wish. The child pounces on a box tied up with a ribbon. When he opens the lid he finds a small tin violin.

'Lovely,' the boy rejoices and tries to play it straight away.

The festivities are, however, interrupted by some banging on the door. Outside stands a woman with a man's briefcase, pressing a hand to her heart.

'D'you have to live so high up?' she pants.

Before Louka can say anything, the stranger threateningly introduces herself: 'I am Zubatá. Social Welfare Department. May I come in?'

The lady with the alarming name – Zubatá means big-toothed in Czech – puts her briefcase on the table, pulls out some papers from it and sits down without being invited to do so.

'You wrote to us, Mr Louka. An application, because you're looking after the boy on your own. There are lots of cases like that, you understand, so we've only just got round to you now.'

Louka is getting worried.

'But that was a long time ago. In the meantime things . . .'

'Just so. You're not the only one and we can't process everything at once. You're a musician. Do you play at night?'

'No. Exclusively during the day. I wrote that letter at a time when . . .'

'You state in your application that you play at night. So you're saying, during the day.' She corrects the entry. 'Where does the child sleep?'

'We both sleep here.' Louka points to his bed.

'He has no bed of his own or a nursery room?'

'No, but there's plenty . . . I had it made extra wide so that . . .'

'He hasn't.' Zubatá ticks her notes.

'Look here, Mrs Zubatá, I wrote that letter at a time when I had a lot on my plate, you understand . . .' Louka would have liked to cancel the whole business but the official pursues her own line:

'The child has Russian nationality, doesn't he? Stop playing now, boy!'

'Yes, but by now he understands quite a lot of Czech and sometimes even . . .'

'The mother has emigrated to the West, isn't that so, and is showing no interest in the child.'

'Oh yes, she is. She's apparently applied through the Red Cross,' Louka points out, but the official doesn't seem to be interested.

'Look here, Mr Lučina, the matter stands like this. Even if by marrying you the mother acquired Czech citizenship, this does not release her from her original Russian one, you understand. In other words, the Soviet embassy is interested in the child. They're keeping a sharp eye on these things. This means the whole business will bypass us and they'll presumably find a place for the boy in some children's home in the Soviet Union. At least that's how I see it.'

Louka goes rigid. Kolya, as though again sensing danger, climbs on to his lap.

Kolya towers above the level of the crowd because Louka has taken him on his shoulders. Also demonstrating on their left is Louka's friend Houdek (Ladislav Smoljak).

'Mrs Zubatá. This letter of mine, couldn't it be revoked?'

'Why revoke it? They'll look after the boy.' Mrs Zubatá shuts her briefcase and gets up.

'I'll be coming again, Mr Lučina . . .'

'Louka,' František corrects her.

'Very well, I'll be coming again, and that'll be with someone from the embassy, and they'll be channelling things their way. Handsome boy.' She has at last looked at the object of her business, and gets ready to leave.

When the door has shut behind her Louka begins to walk in silence up and down his tower room, from the cello to the window and back again.

Kolya's eyes follow him questioningly.

Then Louka halts and their eyes meet.

Decided.

Louka pulls a chair up to the wardrobe. On top of it is a large suitcase.

'*Chemodan?*' Kolya asks in surprise as Louka heaves it down.

'*Chemodan,*' Louka replies. 'Before that Zubatá woman comes to get us.'

The headlights of Louka's Trabant sweep along the Karlovy Vary road. Kolya is asleep in the back, while Louka reflects on what chances of success this attempted flight can have. A rabbit is caught in the headlights, the brakes squeal, and the rabbit escapes with his life.

'Frank?' Houdek is amazed to see him. Houdek is a slight man of forty and he is no stranger to us because we met him passing along the pavement while Louka was cleaning the guttering at his parental home. Wearing a sweatshirt and tracksuit trousers he delightedly unlocks his front door. His amazement grows when he sees the small boy.

'Hi. Can you put us up for a night? We have sleeping bags.'

'Sure as hell,' the ambushed friend replies and admits his nocturnal visitors.

In a small room two armchairs are pushed together to make a bed for Kolya. Louka puts him into his sleeping bag. Their host covers him up with a blanket.

'The sofa here has nasty springs, but when they are covered with a blanket they don't push through.'

'This uncle here is called Houdek,' Louka informs Kolya. 'Although you'll probably call him Goudek. Would you believe it, they can't pronounce an "h" to save their lives. A great power like that, and they can't pronounce an "h",' he adds for Houdek's benefit.

The bottle of wine is almost empty and the two friends have practically told each other everything.

'What a fool you are.' Houdek, lightly oiled, shakes his head. 'Just proves that every marriage is a disaster, even a sham one.'

'They'll track us down anyway, that's child's play for them,' says Louka, scratching his beard.

'No, they won't. D'you know how much they have on their hands right now? They're in the shit left, right and centre. I'll hide you here like parachutists. At least I'll have some illegal activity to my credit. I wanted to sign that Charter thing, but nobody had it here. Have you got it?'

'No. D'you think Nováček will take me on?' Louka asks.

'Bound to. Except he'll think it a little strange that a virtuoso like Louka wants to join a spa orchestra. We'll tell him – Christ, that's a good idea – we'll tell him that you're convalescing here after a gall-bladder operation. You'll be quaffing that Gagarin water all the time. Hell, this illegal activity is fun . . .' Houdek finishes his glass and rubs his hands in a peculiar way: he folds them as in prayer, then he rubs them against each other faster and faster until he can go no faster.

The promenade orchestra on the colonnade plays all the great favourites.

*'When will you visit us?' the boy asks in a mixture
of Czech and Russian.*

Just now it is Dvořák's Slavonic Dance No. 2. Louka's cello is placed between two neighbours. A wind is blowing and he therefore has his music held open by a clothes peg. Among the clarinets we recognize his friend Houdek. On the box next to the conductor sits Kolya, holding a spa mug with a drinking spout and listening.

He is observing the *art nouveau* colonnade, the spa buildings and the visitors.

When the piece is finished and applause breaks out, Kolya runs over to Louka with the little beaker of health-giving water.

Nováček the conductor waits for the maestro to have his drink and only then taps his baton for the next piece.

When Nováček turns to the woodwinds Louka secretly spits out the Gagarin spring under his chair.

Kolya is sleeping. Houdek and Louka are likewise in their pyjamas and over a final bottle of good-night beer are listening to Radio Free Europe.

'. . . had closed Národní and the adjoining streets, so there was no escape from the area. Face to face with the armed police the students chanted: "We have only our bare hands" and sang the national anthem, but they were nevertheless brutally clubbed. On International Students' Day blood flowed in Prague.'

'I'd hate to be wrong, Frank, but I think the balloon has just gone up,' remarks Houdek.

'You're an odd customer. There they are beating people about their heads . . .' Louka tries to contradict him, but Houdek stops him:

'Hang on! Quiet!'

'The students of Prague's higher education institutions are calling on all fellow citizens to join their protest,' the announcer continues.

'A pity, isn't it, that we conducted our resistance from so far away and for such a short time.' Houdek rubs his hands in his own peculiar way. 'The balloon's gone up. And we should have been there, Frank, because, believe me, that's it. It's happening.'

The crowd in the packed St Wenceslas Square roars: 'It's happening! It's happening!'

The priest Malý speaks into the microphone: 'Thank you for making way for the ambulance.'

'Our pleasure! Our pleasure,' the square merrily chants.

Kolya towers above the level of the crowd because Louka has taken him on his shoulders. He has a key bunch in his hands and tinkles it.

Louka looks about him. On his left, clarinet under his arm, is Houdek, standing on tiptoe and rubbing his hands at an alarming speed. Behind him there is a bunch of secondary schoolboys and to their right there are hospital nurses in their blue-and-white uniforms. They all ring their keys over their heads. Looking at them Louka suddenly freezes. Against this ringing-out of the old dispensation he suddenly hears the voice of his fingerless uncle Růžička.

'But at home nobody wanted them back, and especially the young people and the hospital nurses rebelled, and so, with all bells ringing, they drove them out and established a reservation for them in Albania, like the Red Indians. That's the vision he had.'

Before Louka recovers from his astonishment at the way this prophecy has so splendidly come true, he experiences an even greater astonishment. In front of him in the crowd he catches sight of nice Captain Pokorný and nasty Captain Novotný. Both are holding their hands aloft and ringing the keys from their offices at Secret Police headquarters. Nasty Captain Novotný, whose eyes are intently sweeping the crowds, notices Louka and nods his head at him with a smile. Whether this is intended as a salute or a threat he doesn't know himself yet.

And then the revolutionary crowd starts singing 'Oh, my dear son', the favourite song of old Masaryk, the late founder of the Republic. Houdek enlivens it by joining in with his clarinet. On the dais a short man shyly steps up to the microphone. He doesn't know yet that he will be President.

From the viewing platform of Prague airport Louka and Kolya are looking down expectantly on the runway. Now Louka is pointing into the distance.

Andrey Khalimon and Zdeněk Svěrák in a break between takes.

A Lufthansa plane has touched down on Czech soil and smoke rises around its undercarriage.

Hand in hand they run down to the arrivals hall to make sure they don't miss her.

Nadezhda Bilyukova appears in the turnstile. She is a beautiful woman in western clothes. Her eyes, in which both fear and joy are present, roam over the groups of those waiting there.

At last she spots them. Louka nudges Kolya to run and meet his mother, but the boy suddenly doesn't want to. Maybe she seems changed to him or maybe the situation is too much for him, but there is a block. Kolya drops his head and makes no move. In the end he even turns and buries his face in Louka's coat.

Louka has to turn him round by force so his mother can embrace him. The woman in the western clothes starts lamenting in Russian and streams of tears soak Kolya's shoulder.

Later they are drinking coffee in the airport restaurant. Through the big window Kolya watches a large aircraft being unloaded.

'I thank you once more,' Nadezhda says in Russian, 'and hope you'll forgive me.' She strokes the back of his hand, then reaches into her handbag and on the table before Louka lies an open envelope in which he glimpses a stack of German banknotes.

Louka pushes it back to Nadezhda.

A loudspeaker asks passengers for Frankfurt to prepare for boarding.

Before the customs gate Louka hands Nadezhda the suitcase with Kolya's things and for a moment sits down by his side.

'Ahoy,' he says in a tight voice and kisses him.

'Agoy. When will you visit us?' the linguistically corrupted boy asks in a mixture of Czech and Russian.

Louka is unable to say anything more, so he just nods and for a last time strokes Kolya's hair.

The Trabant, the only thing left to Louka from his entire marital adventure, is driving away from the airport. Like the great bird Noh who carries off little children the aircraft thunders overhead, its underbelly flashing in the sun.

Louka inadvertently looks behind him. There really is no one there. He is once more on his own.

Prague has lived to see another spring. Pedestrians are walking about, the trams are running, the sun is shining.

Outside the half-ajar circular window three pigeons are strutting about the warm roof-tiles, waiting for it to be opened.

In the Old Town Square sits a symphony orchestra, playing Smetana's *My Country*. The elderly gentleman with a flowing white mane behind his ears is Rafael Kubelík, who has returned from voluntary exile. The audience surrounds the orchestra on all sides. Quite close, to make sure she can see the musicians, stands Klára Koutská. Does her belly project rather more than it used to? It does.

Among the cellists with their vibrating left hands on the necks of their instruments sits František Louka, in a dinner jacket with a festive bow-tie at his neck. If we look more closely, right on to his sheet music, we find that clamped to it with a clothes peg is a photograph of a small boy with a red bus in his hand and a forced smile on his face.

LIMERICK COUNTY LIBRARY

Director Jan Svěrák with director of photography Vladimir Smutný.

WITHDRAWN FROM STOCK